The Author

GABRIELLE ROY was born in St. Boniface, Manitoba, in 1909. Her parents were part of the large Quebec emigration to western Canada in the late nineteenth century. The youngest of eight children, she studied in a convent school for twelve years, then taught school herself, first in isolated Manitoba villages and later in St. Boniface.

In 1937 Roy travelled to Europe to study drama, and during two years spent in London and Paris she began her writing career. The approaching war forced her to return to Canada, and she settled in Montreal.

Roy's first novel, *The Tin Flute*, ushered in a new era of realism in Quebec fiction with its compassionate depiction of a working-class family in Montreal's Saint-Henri district. Her later fiction often turned for its inspiration to the Manitoba of her childhood and her teaching career.

In 1947 Roy married Dr. Marcel Carbotte, and after a few years in France, they settled in Quebec City, which was to remain their home. Roy complemented her fiction with essays, reflective recollections, and three children's books. Her many honours include three Governor General's Awards, France's Prix Fémina, and Quebec's Prix David.

Gabrielle Roy died in Quebec City, Quebec, in 1983.

Gabrielle Roy

WINDFLOWER

Translated by Joyce Marshall

With an Afterword by Phyllis Webb

M&S

La Rivière sans repos
Original edition
Copyright © 1970 by Gabrielle Roy
Windflower
Translated by Joyce Marshall
Copyright © 1970 by Gabrielle Roy
Afterword copyright © 1991 by Phyllis Webb

First published in English in 1970 by McClelland and Stewart

Reprinted 1994

Canadian Cataloguing in Publication Data

Roy, Gabrielle, 1909–1983
[Rivière sans repos. English]
Windflower

(New Canadian library)
Translation of: La rivière sans repos.
Includes bibliographical references.
ISBN 0-7710-9879-0

I. Title. II. Title: Rivière sans repos. English.
III. Series.

PS8535.095R513 1991   C843'.54   C91-094385-0
PQ3919.R74R513 1991

The characters and events in this novel are fictitious. Any resemblance they have to people and events in life is purely coincidental.

Printed and bound in Canada

McClelland & Stewart Inc.
The Canadian Publishers
481 University Avenue
Toronto, Ontario
M5G 2E9

WINDFLOWER

ONE

1

The rugged land, so naked under its persistent sky, had no shelter anywhere to offer love. Even the summer night, which scarcely darkens here, was not a refuge.

Over towards the white men's village, it was true, there was the old hangar abandoned by the air charter company, with its tumbledown roof, but two fierce dogs had just been posted there.

The Eskimo parents themselves, with their indulgent natures, might not have offered much opposition to meetings between their daughters and the young Americans stationed in the region. But where could they be together? The cabins almost never contained a bedroom or even a real bed. Lovemaking must be conducted, most of the time, in haste, under the derisive eye of some witness. Deprived of mystery, it was thus, here even more than elsewhere, reduced to what is said to be its essential. Human beings coupled at times like the animals, as they chanced to meet, on the harsh moss of the tundra, exposed to the pitiless sky.

Some of the bolder GI's had tried, with the connivance of the sentries, to bring girls into their barracks. This had gone so badly for them that even the Eskimo parents had been startled. Such a punishment for something that was after all only natural!

So the pure terrible country, which lies open from one end to the other had, you might say, neither time nor place favourable to love. Except, in a pinch, the faint dip in the ground midway between the army barracks and the Eskimo village that stretched at some length along the shore of the Koksoak River. In this partly sheltered hollow a little earth, come from no one knew where, had gathered through the years. Not very much, just a fine scanty layer, but grasses had eventually managed to take root there and, later, trees. Trees? Well, poor midget trees, small sickly creatures, at once childish-looking and very old, wrinkled all over. On the other hand, they grew stiflingly close, they too driven by that inexorable law of nature: the more hostile the conditions, the fiercer the struggle to multiply.

There was little advantage, however, in going right into this thicket, for, once within it, though finally shielded from the staring of the sky, you were at the mercy of the most cunning scourge of that inhuman country: at the heart of these damp rotting bushes was the domain of incessantly breeding insects.

Even so, when a year or two had passed since a detachment of the American army had come to this little lost post of Fort Chimo, a fairly large number of children of mixed blood was born in the Eskimo village.

Among these births there was one as dazzling to the people of the region as the appearance in their sky of a new star.

In testimony then, here is the story, just as it is told in those parts, of Elsa, daughter of Archibald and Winnie Kumachuk.

With three other young Eskimo girls she was returning one evening, in the extended twilight, from the movie hall where Father Eugene provided two shows a week: one for the whites, one for the Eskimos — best not to mix the groups.

Ever since they left the Catholic mission, the girls had not once stopped laughing, teasing, and chattering, and the immense, silent, almost empty land, as sonorous as a huge drum, reverberated into the distance with this youthful gayety.

They had their arms linked as they had seen girls do in the movies and walked abreast at a good pace along the wide tarred road the Army had just built to connect its barracks with the airstrip. This road was not long, just slightly over a mile, after which came the same rough bumpy soil as always where, even by walking in the same places for years, no one had ever managed to mark out anything faintly resembling a path. But probably because it was very short, the effect of this smooth surface was extraordinary. You felt all at once that you were somewhere else, perhaps in a city. The girls loved this road and came there on the slightest pretext. So it had become to some extent the "boardwalk" of Fort Chimo. The girls had nowadays even forsaken the old pleasant walk beside the river, where they used to spend hours at a time searching for those flat stones that can be skipped on the water.

But that was all in the past. Now they went to the movies and, their heads full of romantic stories, talked about them endlessly, in an effort to unravel the plots or just simply to laugh. In fact, love stories or frivolous comedies, tales of espionage or musical fantasies all seemed to them almost equally comic.

This evening they were discussing an old Clark Gable movie. Unlike many of the world's film-goers, they had found Gable himself extremely ugly but, to make up for this, incomparably funny when he kissed the heroine.

As they tried to figure out the plot of this love story, with its incredible vicissitudes, they were climbing with matched steps up a small rise in the road.

Above them the sky still held, despite the lateness of the hour, a tinge of dull gold. It was the daily festival, the moment of magic, the strange spectacle the austere land provides for itself almost every summer evening. The girls reached the top of the little hill. Now they were outlined in black against the glowing sky. Often in those regions such small human friezes form on the rim of the horizon, visible from far away and, though tiny, captured and revealed in every detail.

So one could have recognized, even at a fair distance, the four silhouettes, almost identical, all rather short and round, of Elsa, Mary Jane, Lily, and Mildred.

Since they were returning from "town," they were dressed in their very best – a rather commonplace best compared to the parkas and pretty sealskin boots of former times. Nowadays they wore short dresses of flowered cotton, over which floated sweaters as shapeless as sacks. On their feet, at this season that was dry enough to crack stones, were rubber boots – a type of footgear so much in vogue in the Eskimo country that the stores could not keep up with the demand, the more so as the boots were worn out in no time by the jaggedness of a soil for which they were not intended. Nothing, however, could prevent these laughing young creatures from being charming with their rounded cheeks and short tight braids as they were profiled that evening against the twilight, all still busy unravelling the meaning of the film they had seen. It seemed unbelievable, up here on the edge of the Arctic, this story of the South with its giant trees and its lawns upon which sank romantic women in silk dresses yielding to endless kisses.

"Ugh!" said Mary Jane, "I sure wouldn't like to be mouth to mouth with a stranger!"

"You'd need to have a lot of confidence to do it," said Elsa dreamily.

The fever of the twilight was beginning to diminish by a tone. Soon it would be a little dark. The asphalt road went on a bit farther and then the girls must continue along the beach, which was scattered at intervals with the shacks of the Eskimo village.

"I can't really believe people embrace in that intimate way," said Mary Jane again.

Lily also had doubts and even Mildred, more or less, though ordinarily she had no ideas of her own.

Only Elsa maintained her point of view that, strange as it looked to them, elsewhere in the world kissing on the mouth might seem perfectly natural. They had never been there to judge. In any case, she finally announced, half serious, half mocking, she would be quite willing to try it herself if only to find out what it was like. The others scoffed, digging at her with their elbows.

They reached the point where they must separate, the others turning to the right, Elsa to continue straight ahead, along the river.

"Are you afraid? Do you want us to go with you?" suggested the amiable Mary Jane.

Afraid! The very thought that in her own country, under the sky that had always seen her pass, an Eskimo girl could feel threatened would have made them laugh not so long ago. But after all the injunctions from the clergyman and the priest never to walk along the road alone when it was late or loiter on their way home from the village, and the stories of abductions at the movies, a sort of nervousness sometimes slipped for an instant into their gentle and placid souls. But this was not properly speaking anxiety. Under all that ever-present sky who could be so uneasy?

Elsa refused her companions' offer pleasantly. Once she had skirted the sombre group of little trees, the landscape would be brightened again by the diffused light of the Koksoak, which drew closer here, swelling into one of its broad indentations. Already, moreover, she could hear its murmuring very clearly. She listened to it intently. Though she loved the cinema as a marvellous dream, she was equally gladdened by the mere fact of returning to the realities of the Eskimo country: these scattered rickety huts, the path that approached them along the beach and especially the river, whose murmur had been part of things always, ever since she had been in the world. From where she stood she could distinguish in the distance, mirrored in the water, a handful of tiny glimmerings among which were the lights of her own home. In the blink of an eye she had formed the simple familiar image of her family, so cramped together in the hut that they gave an impression of warm intimacy: the grandfather tirelessly carving some little figure or gesture of the old days from soapstone, as if he must prevent its memory at least from being lost; the father dismantling and reassembling the old, always broken-down motor of his fishing boat; the mother so happy to live in a real house instead of a tent or an igloo that she gazed around it again and again, meanwhile giving herself hearty slaps of contentment upon the thighs.

Elsa, who was the most impatient to run to the cinema, was also the most anxious always to return home.

"Bye-bye," she called to her friends and set off at a bound.

The boy was suffering, concealed in the shade of the thicket, a handkerchief pressed to his face to protect it from bites. Black, famished, and strident, the mosquitoes gyrated madly, forming a sort of nimbus around him. What was worst about this hell of waiting? The stifling heat, the lack of air or, whenever he lowered his mask to breathe, the immediate attack of the mosquitoes? He had never seen any so huge. In this so-called cold country, his most persistent reason for astonishment was its violent heat, which he complained of again and again in letters to his family in Mississippi: "Cripes! would you believe it? It can get as hellishly hot here as it does back home."

In a muffled voice he cursed the heat, the mosquitoes and perhaps, unconsciously, the ardour of his youth, which was goading him as cruelly as it does all life during the brief Arctic summer.

He heard the voices of Elsa's companions diminish while she herself drew nearer. Peaceful and yet strong, the murmuring of the river rose through the calm air like distant gentle voices joined in an indistinct song. Suddenly Elsa appeared. Her two tight braids bounced on her shoulders with the rhythm of her bounding walk. With her wide beaming face, strongly marked cheekbones and rather short legs, the Eskimo girl had little, despite the fine vivacity of her expression, to please the young soldier from the South. But soon it would grow darker, and she looked clean, at least.

He stretched out a hand to stop her.

"Hi, baby."

She could not see much of him, since he still kept his face half-hidden and his forage cap was pulled well down over his forehead. However, she greeted him kindly.

"Hi, soldier."

She had time only to be astonished that, even with the daylight gone, he was still wearing his sun-glasses. For he was already pulling her into the bushes. He pressed his mouth against her lips.

All she would ever really know of him, then, was that he was young and had a heart that beat as madly as that of a wild creature in a trap.

Aside from this panic, however, everything was just like the movies, strange, removed, scarcely believable. In the centre of the spindly copse there was a small, slightly trodden-down circle. A deer had perhaps come here to sleep or suffer. Unless other couples before. . . .

The soldier pushed Elsa down and fell upon her.

Then the cloud of mosquitoes, swelling from second to second, descended upon them. (But what did they live on when there was no blood of humans or animals to drink?) Elsa's skin was used to their bites. But the GI, who from what she could see at wrists and neck had a delicate, pink flesh, must be suffering cruelly. He was swearing. He interrupted himself to drive away the insects with broad sweeping gestures. He must have been breathing them through his nostrils, perhaps swallowing them, for he was seized by a fit of coughing. He was strangling. Elsa could not keep from laughing a little. The GI silenced her with a hand over her mouth as if this childish laughter humiliated him profoundly. He was neither rough nor brutal, merely in a hurry. Even Elsa's parents did not go more quickly. This was perhaps why she was so

8

dazed she could scarcely separate the reality of the bushes from the love story she had seen on the screen earlier in the evening, of which this seemed the sequel.

The end, however, was very different. The GI was even more impatient to get out of the bushes than he had been to push her in, for they were pursued by insects that were now as thick as smoke.

At the edge of the little thicket he took just time enough to mumble something. Thank you? Good-bye? Elsa did not catch the words since they were spoken so quickly into the handkerchief in an accent she had never heard. At the same time he pressed a few bills into her hand. Then he departed at a run along the shore.

She stood there for a moment, watching his flight.

He stopped, though, before he took the turning towards the camp. But he was now too far away for her to distinguish anything but a slender silhouette against the darkened skyline.

However, elbow against his body, he made a little movement of the hand in Elsa's direction.

And it had every appearance of a friendly gesture.

2

Of this episode on a July evening beside the murmuring Koksoak little might have remained but some images as blurred as those of the cinema, swift to be wiped from Elsa's mind, if her body had not undergone a physical change. A few more months and this change became apparent.

She herself seemed neither depressed nor pleased. It was a thing that happened. That it should happen before marriage caused no discredit here. Rather the contrary. Elsa's parents displayed no indignation. They confined themselves to teasing her: So she'd been in a hurry to taste it, had she?

Winter closed the family in together. In the centre of the airtight cabin roared the stove that burned oil delivered by ship in summer at enormous expense. The mother had managed to obtain a length of multicoloured cotton and was making herself an ample dress for the festivities of the winter. The father had put away the engine of his boat for good and was mending an old fishing net. At a crate placed upright, Elsa's little brother sat doing his homework. He could be heard repeating scraps of strange lessons learned at school, such as: The cat purrs. A cat no one hereabouts had ever seen.

Old Thaddeus, for his part, had begun with the onset of winter to carve the familiar snowy owls of the region with their strongly curved beaks. Now and then, as if seeking inspiration, he would raise his head, listening to the wind shaking the cabin, then continue to release the bird from the soft stone. For a long time he had been the only one in this family who sometimes lost himself in thoughts of which he did not speak. Now Elsa more and more resembled her grandfather in her expression of attentiveness to something within herself.

Archibald, her father, and Winnie, her mother, found this a subject for jokes.

"There she goes wandering off again! Is she searching for her sweetheart, do you suppose?"

Elsa would shrug and look away, showing some ill-humour. For there was this change in her at least: from the laughing girl she had been, she had become rather morose and withdrawn.

Her parents told themselves it might be better to leave her alone.

In the end there was only the Reverend Hugh Paterson, the Anglican pastor, to take Elsa's condition really to heart.

He met her one day on the shore of the great river, whose murmuring was now buried under the heavy weight of ice. She was standing there as if absorbed in thought or perhaps aimless, her eyes vague, shivering with the cold in her old worn-out boots. A few weeks before at church he had observed that all did not seem to be well with Elsa. She no longer listened to God's word with the same fresh confident attitude as of old.

Now he saw very clearly how it was with her and he was indignant.

"Who did this to you, Elsa?"

It could not have been a young man of her own people, for he would have immediately asserted his right to the fruit of the union.

"Then it was one of the GI's?"

She answered neither yes nor no, her gaze wandering indifferently as if she were quite outside all this.

"Did he force you?'"

She turned her eyes back to the tall gaunt man. "No."

In all honesty she could not say he had forced her, not much in any case.

"You mean that you consented, Elsa? You didn't defend yourself?"

She shook her head. That wasn't it either. She had not, as he put it, consented. . . . The whole thing was really becoming too tangled. She turned away her eyes to gaze far into the heaped-up ice that was all that now marked what had been a great flow of free and singing water. Why should this event of a few minutes be given so much importance now? And did she know whether or not she had really defended herself?

"In any case you're a minor. The GI's, moreover, are forbidden by law to associate with the Eskimo girls. And did I not tell you repeatedly as well," he concluded, raising his voice, "to keep away from the soldiers?"

"I did keep away from them," said Elsa in the tone of a reprimanded child who still has some excuse to offer for herself.

The pastor's anger subsided somewhat. He too seemed depressed.

"Tell me his name, Elsa."

She resumed her study of the distant blocks of ice with their peculiar shapes. Her face was once more apathetic. She nudged at a stone with her foot.

"I don't know what it is."

"You don't even know his name!"

She shrugged.

"He didn't tell me."

Besides, what would that change? If she knew his name, would she know him better?

"At least you know what he looked like?"

Her expression was weary. She wasn't even too sure of that.

"He had, I think, blue eyes," she said.

"Blue eyes," the pastor repeated. "And what else?"

"Perhaps blond hair."

"That's a great help," he said. "Listen, Elsa. When the GI's come to the village or march out as a group, try to post yourself where you can watch them pass. Examine them as they go by and then come and describe to me the. . . ."

He could not bring himself to say "the father" or "the lover"; neither of these words suited. And he found "the guilty one" also distasteful now that there was to be a child. Could that be said: guilty of having a child?

Almost without expression, she whose face had always been so lively, Elsa said quietly, "But if I recognize him and he doesn't recognize me."

"That is not the point," said the pastor. "Listen to me again, Elsa. This boy is more responsible than you for what is happening. He must be forced at the very least to help you bring up the child. And finally we must make an example. . . ."

An example! Did not this mean essentially: punish? Even more: take one from among several and punish that one alone.

She said she would think about it and went off with dragging steps along the beach.

Neither the next day nor the day afterwards did she feel any inclination to go and station herself where the squad of soldiers went by in fair weather or foul, urged along the road by their sergeant's shouts of left, right, left, right . . . through the gusts of wind.

It came about rather by chance.

One day, when she was returning from the Hudson's Bay store where she had made some small purchases for her mother, she heard the measured tramp of the squad coming briskly along behind her over the squeaking snow. Her first thought was simply to yield way, so she stepped to one side, sinking into the soft snow. When the squad was close, she remembered the pastor's advice and dared to raise her eyes timidly towards the group as it marched past. She searched for blue eyes and almost all were blue. For light hair and what could be seen below the forage caps was light. Young features, and all were young. She blinked her eyes a little in the powdery snow raised by their steps and perhaps for the first time in her life felt ridiculous and alone.

Suddenly however, in the middle of the squad, a glance lowered as soon as it had met her own and seemed trying to escape. The other boys had tossed her a free indifferent look as they passed. Only this one appeared constrained. Was this he? As soon as she had recognized him, the pastor had said, she need only point him out to the soldier in command. Yet she remained hesitant. The eyes of the young GI met hers again in a strange sidelong look that seemed to be imploring her not to do him any harm. She remembered the excited heart that had beat against her own in great rapid thuds. She remembered above all the sketchy but touching gesture at the turning of the beach, against the darkening sky.

Besides, was she sure she was not mistaken? Her face dull, she let the squad pass without her features really changing expression. When the snow had settled, she followed some distance after the soldiers, her steps slow. The road at the present time was kept open all winter even during storms. But Elsa no longer cared for this road and if she still sometimes walked there this was only out of habit or because she was too lazy to beat a path for herself.

From that day on it was no longer possible to get the least word from her about the matter.

Silent, like a marmot on the point of hibernation, Elsa seemed to have no interest in anything and none at all in the child she would soon bring into the world.

"At least," the pastor enjoined her, "let the nurse examine you. Don't neglect yourself and the child."

She gave that little pout that came to her lips now whenever anyone spoke to her for what they called "her own good."

However, like the white women, who always made such a great fuss about having a baby, she submitted, as she might have to a play, to regular visits to the nurse, the monthly weighing, and blood and urine tests.

At one time she would at least have laughed at all this. Now she was neither amused nor really annoyed. Very little, seemingly, could touch her.

It was in this state of mind that she came to her time. On foot, her bundle in her arms, in her boots that were now almost in shreds, she set out along the road that a crew of soldiers had just cleared after a night of heavy gusts.

She gave birth without a whimper, her face scarcely discomposed, gazing steadily at the ceiling. And then, abruptly, everything changed for her. It hap-

pened at the precise moment when Mademoiselle
Bourgoin, the head nurse, thrust the child almost
forcibly into her arms.

"Just look at him," she said. "Such a beautiful little
boy!"

Elsa looked, and what she saw caught her by surprise, took her breath away so completely it seemed
it would never be restored.

Her expression at that moment was like the sky of
her country when it has long been empty and then,
accompanied by delicate clouds and a mild wind,
comes the first flight of confident birds from the south.
Her soul, so long absent, glowed in her eyes again but
larger now, more loving and more wondering.

So it seemed to everyone that in giving life to her
child she had restored her own life to herself.

3

But if at her first look at this child with the light eyes and pale hair who had come from herself, so swarthy, she had felt herself sink into bottomless depths of love, how can one speak of her marvelling when at about six months he had reached his full splendour of dimpled pink babyhood.

His eyes were the blue of those glimpses of sky between the snowy April clouds. His hair, as silky as the down on baby ducks, was already long. Elsa could give herself up for hours to the pleasure of rolling it on her fingers as she had seen Madame Beaulieu do with her baby's hair at the time when Elsa had worked for that lady, not even dreaming then that she was learning a gesture that one day would be useful to herself. But, it is true, life was essentially one surprise after another.

Just the same! Hair that curled! Elsa touched her own hair, which now seemed to her clumsy, heavy and stiff, then she touched her son's, making her hand very gentle and smiling all over her face. She began to remake the little crest of golden hair, endeavouring to show it off better and give it still more softness and lightness. The child himself, who had not yet become impatient with his young mother of the dark face who was forever washing and combing him, for the moment offered no resistance, even laughed with her at times.

One day she put on his prettiest clothes and went out to display him to the world. That is to say she took him to the "hall" of the Catholic mission, a room in his own house that Father Eugene had put at the disposal of the Eskimos so they could drop in from time to time and perhaps stay to smoke, or read, or play cards. There was always someone there. But this evening, when Elsa came in with her baby, the room was crowded. Trying to look modest, despite the pride blazing in her eyes, she seated herself a little to one side, on a backless bench along the wall, and sat her child on her knee, supporting his back with the flat of her hand. He was all in pale blue. In her choice of clothes for him as in everything else now, Elsa took advice from no one but the white people and on this point Mademoiselle Bourgoin had been emphatic: girls in pink, boys in blue.

Remarkable already for his features, the baby was even more so for his clothing, which seemed very odd to the other mothers with children on their knees or standing beside them, each dressed in very nearly the entire spectrum of colours.

Everyone in the hall had his eyes riveted upon this extraordinary child. The little fellow, who sat very erect, jiggling slightly on his mother's lap, wrinkled his brows as he considered the dark faces that surrounded him. Suddenly he raised his hands and began to beat them together as if in applause, his whole body shaken with irresistible merriment. His laughter was fresh and mocking. It was as if he were trying to say: "Goodness, but I've landed in a funny world!"

At that moment the child Jimmy so conquered the hearts of the Eskimo people that afterwards he could always do with them whatever he wanted.

The women present and even the men then asked Elsa if they couldn't, as a great favour, hold her son for a moment, rock him a little, and coax him to smile. Passed from arm to arm, he began to circle the room. Elsa followed him with her eyes, smiling and finding it very difficult not to look too proud. All she wanted was to be avenged for the time when she had walked through the cold in her worn-out boots and received sarcastic or pitying looks as she passed.

Poor Emily, as black as a prune with sagging breasts, held the blond child pressed against her for a moment. Then it was the turn of the very ancient Aurora who strained her weak eyes, trying to make out, through the haze in which she lived, the little top-knot of hair. "Look, Grandmother, his hair is as fine as the crest of a bird." Then Thalia . . . then little Edwin, only five himself but determined to imitate the grown-ups and see what they saw. Then old Elias as in the story of another old man, in a temple. . . until, suddenly impatient, the baby clenched his fists and burst into sharp sobs. Elsa then took her son and retired as best she could to the back of the hall. Turned slightly away from the company, she gave her child the breast, patting his buttocks like an experienced mother well versed already in the art of pacifying the young. She was crooning an old lullaby, so old no one could remember when it had been born — during a night of violent storm perhaps on the infinite ocean of the tundra, in some little snow house as alone and lost as a dune among dunes.

She might, however, have been sorry later that she had perhaps unconsciously tried to make the women jealous when she began to find them turning up at all hours, sometimes one, sometimes another, entreating and stubborn, to see whether she wouldn't let them borrow Jimmy "at least for a quarter of an hour."

"You have children yourselves," she would retort, flattered but severe. "Rock and cuddle them as much as you like."

Certainly they had children and loved them dearly just as they were with their little dark faces, their hair as flat and stiff as sticks, and their coal-black mischievous eyes.

But to hold this unique little being in their arms was quite a different matter. They did not know how to express it . . . it seemed to them that it was holding much more in their arms than was usual on earth.

"I don't want you to spoil him," said Elsa, "and make him impossible for me to handle."

Yet if she did not often consent to "lend" her son, she was quite willing for them to come, each on her own, to admire him as much as they liked in the family hut.

This hut was changing as much as Elsa herself. Who would have recognized it from the time when everyone used to sit dreaming on his own side, Elsa most of all, letting everything lie where it fell – animal guts, food, clothing – so that on Sunday morning they had to spend a good hour searching among the rags and tatters and under the benches for something to put on so they could set out, fresh and clean, towards the church to meet the Lord. True, soon no one would know Archibald and Winnie's old hut.

With her grandfather's help she had put some shelves in two wooden crates that had once contained lard, added a piece of plastic as a curtain and thus had two nice little cupboards for her own and her son's clothes. There was enough flowered plastic left to frame the windows. She had then cleared away a corner to make a bedroom for the two of them behind a bearskin suspended from the ceiling. Here even more than elsewhere it was forbidden to spit on the floor or admit the flea-infested dogs.

Though the neighbours had first laughed at these changes, which they interpreted as so many affectations, they were finally so impressed that, returning to their homes, they suddenly saw the disorder in which they lived and began to make cupboards and curtains for themselves.

But it was the baby's bath that lured the most people to the little house beside the Koksoak.

It was impossible to miss it except on purpose, for Elsa bathed her child at a set hour, as prescribed by Mademoiselle Bourgoin who had been equally firm about this: "Elsa dear, if you want to have a calm and happy child, give him regular habits from the beginning. It's not a matter of washing him when it suits you or you feel the inclination but every day at the same hour."

Of course Mademoiselle Bourgoin could not have suspected that these wise words would, so to speak, oblige a whole population to arrange its life to suit a baby, but this was indeed what came to pass.

Shortly before ten o'clock in the morning, all over the beach along the Koksoak, women would be seen leaving their cabins and setting forth. It was not in the least astonishing to see them almost all outdoors and on the move at the same time, for since they first began to live in a village they had never got over what seemed to them its principal advantage: being able to visit one another all day long, starting early in the morning. What was new was to see them all converging upon the same point.

As one encountered another, they would form little groups moving along the rim of the immense horizon. From far away they could be heard laughing and gossiping. Many of them brought their own children; dogs followed. So the little parade began to give a sort of festival air each day to the most denuded horizon in the world.

Suddenly the women would begin to hurry, concerned lest they be late, because of Elsa's present mania for doing everything by the clock without even consenting to wait a few minutes for those who were on the way.

They would arrive seven or eight at a time, not counting the children, and take their places wherever they could against the wall, some sitting on a bench and the others standing.

The table in the centre of the room had been cleared. Stove, bag of flour, boxes of tea and sugar, and leftover food were all now on the floor below. In truth, in her efforts to have a surface to work on, Elsa was obliged to be always moving things about.

Winnifred, who was easy-going by nature, did not interfere but simply sat among the spectators.

Then the ritual began.

First Elsa carried a white, well-scoured basin from the stove close by. Into this she poured hot water. Next she brought a cake of mild white soap, talcum, and a little hairbrush whose bristles seemed to be made themselves from fine hair.

These objects she laid meticulously on the table. She then gathered her son from a sort of little jute swing with a back-rest and holes for the legs that hung from the low ceiling. She laid him on the table and began to undress him.

When his little sex appeared, tender as a rosebud, the women turned to one another to exchange smiles of complicity. The sight of a small male child always moved them, as it profoundly moves all mothers. Through thoughts of love they were undoubtedly led to reflect upon pleasure and pain, birth and death. The nakedness of Elsa's child struck them anew, however, as if it quickened in them that devouring curiosity of the human heart towards sexuality. If they began by chuckling, at the last they looked grave, their fine dark eyes perplexed.

Perhaps embarrassed by these glances, which had seemed to take stock of her child, Elsa would try to cover him with her hand as she picked him up to put him in the water.

She had already tested its temperature with her elbow as she had seen Madame Beaulieu do with her baby's bath.

A few spiteful souls had gone so far as to point out, and with reason, that Elsa was now copying the very things she had laughed at when she worked for the Beaulieus.

To which Elsa had replied with finality that one often ended in this life by doing what one had originally laughed at in ignorance and that it was not at the moment one laughed but rather at the moment one stopped laughing that one showed the most intelligence.

With the child in the bath, she began to soap him vigorously. He would beat at the water with his hands, making it gush in all directions. His already sonorous laughter filled the wondering silence.

Then came the moment when, having dried the pale hair very carefully, the mother gave herself the satisfaction, before all these gaping women, of demonstrating how easily it could be curled. A flick of the brush against a strand rolled over the finger and that was that: the golden topknot held.

Thus many happy moments slipped by that autumn in the peaceful Eskimo village. But, on the other hand, how many tears were shed afterwards in other cabins! For, as soon as they were home, most of the mothers snatched up their own children and tried to curl their stiff dark hair. The poor children, long-suffering though they might be, had only one thought in their heads these days: to manage somehow to keep out of the way of their mothers. But in this land with its open sky nothing is harder to find, as it happens, than a good place of concealment.

4

The small sum of money the pastor had obtained for her was already used up as was the help her parents had given her and the proceeds from the sale of Thaddeus' carvings which the old man had generously made over to her, and yet Elsa still wakened each morning longing to buy some new article for her child. At present her heart was set on a little blue nylon snowsuit displayed on a plastic baby in the window of the Hudson's Bay – a huge sheet of gleaming glass that stared, one might say, straight at the Arctic Circle. Elsa would slow her steps when she passed, take the few cents she had left out of the pocket of her old sweater, count them one by one, then move on with a disheartened look. It had been useless for the pastor to urge her to avoid this window; Elsa had not the courage. Besides, she would have had to make an enormous detour not to see it, at least in the distance, sparkling quite as much at times as the ocean in the sun. But she had to admit that the pastor was right when he said one could not have everything one wanted in this life and freedom too. She decided to go back to work for Madame Beaulieu as the latter had long been begging her to do. Having made her plan, she went on to action, doubtless fearing that if she put off its execution for just one hour she might change her mind. She set out, her eyes fixed upon the Beaulieu house, which was visible from a long way off. It was very striking. It had been delivered in sections, with doors and windows pre-finished, hoisted up, and assembled on the crest of a rocky knoll. And now it wore, with its big picture windows open upon all this emptiness, a look of considerable astonishment at finding itself here. Elsa never felt very big when she raised her eyes to the high house that had come from the distant city.

Madame Beaulieu, who was standing that afternoon at the wide window in her living-room, as she did very often, had seen and soon recognized Elsa's little silhouette, the only living creature moving at that hour across the barren and pitiless expanse. She went out to meet her, moved, if you could so express it, by a sorrowful joy. In this uttermost end of the earth, to her barbarous, where she was perishing of boredom, even Elsa's company was a gift from heaven.

However, when Elsa understood that to be at Madame Beaulieu's disposal and take care of her children, she would have to forgo keeping an eye on her own child, she almost went straight back home again. She had thought naively that she could bring Jimmy to this fine warm house where he too would be comfortable, a nuisance to no one in his own little corner.

"But you couldn't have thought that, my poor Elsa! One more child to shriek and cry in such a small house!"

To hear this sumptuous dwelling with its four rooms, each possessing doors and windows, called "small" confounded Elsa. Her eyes, which had been gazing around with amazement, lowered to examine her feet in some embarrassment.

But, she suggested timidly, her child was good-tempered and almost never cried.

"So it's said, so it's said," replied Madame Beaulieu plaintively. "But the poor little things always do cry because there's usually something wrong with them somewhere. It's colic or they're cutting teeth. . . . We can only wonder why we bring them into the world — don't you agree, Elsa?"

The large dark eyes, though still trying to smile, became guarded. That was no question to ask oneself, they seemed to be trying to say. And wasn't it because she could ask such a thing of herself that Madame Beaulieu was, as was said in the village, sick in the nerves?

"You must try to be punctual," Madame Beaulieu then said, rather beseechingly, clearly with no great hope of being obeyed.

But on this point Elsa was in complete agreement. She no longer, she said, stayed in bed often till after noon. She had completely changed. She, too, now believed in such things as order, discipline, and always being on time. She even set her little alarm clock every evening.

At the beginning everything went well. Elsa scrubbed and cleaned without being stopped too often by the discouraging thought that tomorrow it would all have to be done again and, besides, it wasn't even on her own behalf. To spend part of one's life, as one must make up one's mind to do, scrubbing and cleaning can when it is at home even be accepted, but when it is in someone else's house, is there an occupation less profitable and more foolish? Elsa plucked up courage by consulting the clock every five minutes and thus verifying the fact that time really was passing and would free her at last to go back to her own home.

However, she was just as painstaking in her care of Madame Beaulieu's children as she was with her own baby, and the two little ones, Carole and André, were already greatly attached to Elsa, watching for her every morning at the big window, which held just the tops of their faces. As she climbed the steps cut into the rock that led up to the house, Elsa was always delighted to see the two smiling faces appear and grow a little more visible at every step.

But unfortunately, even with Elsa nearby, Madame Beaulieu did not recover her spirits. The naked landscape with its distant horizons seemed even so, she said, to close in upon her. But at least she was able to grant Elsa the attention of one prisoner to another prisoner in the same cage.

"Are you fretting?" she asked one day when she found Elsa at the picture window, still dusting away as she glanced from time to time towards the Eskimo village stretched in a long faint stippling upon the whiteness of the snow. "Well then, go," she said. "If you'll promise to come back quickly, you may take a dash down there and make sure that all is well."

Immediately, you might say, Elsa was on her way, struggling to pull on her coat, its sleeves flying behind her. Madame Beaulieu watched a little shape bounding from knoll to knoll, leaving the marks of its steps on the virgin snow, so gathered in upon itself in its efforts to go quickly that it looked like some vague, rolled-up object carried by the wind.

At the Eskimo house the child welcomed his mother but with less joy than she would have wished. He was becoming used to remaining all day with his grandmother Winnie and Thaddeus and was learning to sit quietly for hours on the old man's knee, also gazing into the distance with a sort of contentment.

Then came a morning when he scarcely cried at all as his mother left. Held in the arms of Winnie, who could scarcely conceal her joy at having him all to herself, he waved his hand towards his mother and his face did not pucker into those folds of grief Elsa had found so distressing. She was troubled again as she departed that morning, though not for the usual reason. She realized now that Winnie was going to steal Jimmy right away from her if she did not put a stop to it soon. So it might be better for her to leave everything and stay home to look after him.

But when she had received her first month's wages and run straight to the store, she was dumbfounded to find every cent gone before she noticed. Moreover, she had caught sight of a great many other things she was eager to have. So she thought she would go on working for a little longer.

After a few months of living so much against nature, her eye always on the clock, she began to grow very tired and to lose some of her good nature.

"... it's her fault, all her own fault," Winnie maintained, sitting on the floor, rocking back on her heels.

Elsa stared her down. It was all very well for her mother to be so easy-going; all her life she had been satisfied with what she had and had never tried to improve herself.

Elsa for her part insisted, before she ran to do another woman's housework, upon first doing a little cleaning up at home; above all, she wanted to give her child his bath. But did anyone have a notion what this involved? Just to get the water heated or manage to make a clear space while the cabin was still a dormitory required an uncommon measure of willpower. She must shake this one, who wasn't yet ready to get up, step over another, perform feats of agility, while all the time being careful not to lose her temper.

Winnie, her head tousled, slow to return from her complicated dreams in which she almost always found herself back in the harsh old times, would promise with a yawn that she would wash little Jimmy herself, but later. After all there was no great hurry. . . The child hadn't even had time to get dirty. . . .

"Yes, at the end of the day," Elsa would retort. "When it's no longer worth the trouble."

At such words so early in the morning, when she would have given anything in the world to burrow into her blanket and sleep a while longer, Winnie would find herself wondering whether this was really her daughter. And Elsa, after an unsympathetic examination of poor Winnie, toothless and none too careful of her person, would be telling herself that this woman could not be her mother.

Almost every morning, despite the brief time at their disposal, they would end up in a wrangle — always about progress. Accused of not keeping step with the times, Winnie would finally rebel. She would recall with pride that when she was young she had stood up to her own mother, old Mary, about that very thing. Now there was a woman who wasn't easy. Elsa should have had to deal with her, she would have learned what authority was, but alas, these were soft times, everything was falling apart.

Elsa would leave, somewhat jangled by these discussions, running all the way to recover the time she had lost. Then, in the middle of the day, there would be that other mad race from one house to the other, since Madame Beaulieu had never had the heart to withdraw her permission.

But Elsa insisted upon catching up and always finishing one day's dishes before she started the next day's. This was difficult enough ordinarily, with all the dishes there were in this house; if there hadn't been so many, Elsa thought, there would have been fewer to wash. But on the days when Madame Beaulieu entertained at tea!

The idea was not Elizabeth Beaulieu's own. On the contrary, if, while she sat at her low table serving her guests, she raised her eyes to the picture window through which the pitiless sky came right into the house, she would at once feel judged and found ridiculous, sitting there in front of all that sky, pouring tea and chattering, trying, as the saying goes, to take her mind off herself. This would only deepen her melancholy. But everyone urged her to do her best to defy the formidable power of that desolate land.

So that the little party might have some slight air of festivity, Elsa must don a plain black dress brightened by a white lace-trimmed apron and wear a sort of small crown, also of white lace. Thus adorned, she would run if she had a moment and examine herself from head to foot in the big mirror in Madame Beaulieu's bedroom. A trifle abashed by her reflection but pleased too, she would look at herself for a long time, a wrinkle crossing her forehead and her eyes startled, as if she still were not entirely sure of what she saw. But these were rare moments of reverie that did not leave much trace in her life.

She took pleasure, however, in the preparations for the tea parties: the linen napkins, the delicate cups, the sandwiches made of very white bread, whose crusts were removed though they were just as tender as the crumb. She felt privileged to have an opportunity to learn the refinements of life.

What she liked least was appearing before the ladies burdened with the tea-tray, which she feared might slip at any moment from her hands. These ladies were not strangers to Elsa since she encountered them almost every day of her life, at the store, in the dust of the road, or ankle-deep in snow; but to see them in city dresses seated on Madame Beaulieu's chesterfield gave her the same strange impression as going into the cinema partway through the film.

As soon as she appeared, her hair drawn tightly behind her ears, her brown face shining like pewter, her lips pressed tightly together in her efforts to do everything correctly, the ladies never failed to interrupt their conversation to say, "Hello Elsa. . . How are you Elsa? . . . And your beautiful little boy?"

Elsa would reply that he had cut a tooth or that he was crying a bit at night because of a boil.

Then since the ladies seemed for some incomprehensible reason to be as ill at ease as herself, Elsa would try to dispel some of their awkwardness by enquiring in turn about their children.

They all knew everything about one another in this country without secrecy. Whether one was rich or poor, there was scarcely any way to keep anything to oneself and so the little ritual of questions and answers — Are you well? . . . Why yes, thank you — had an even more melancholy ring here than elsewhere. For either the ladies were acknowledging what was known in the remotest parts of the Eskimo country or they were trying to pretend they were not aware of it . . . and to what purpose?

Elsa would return to the kitchen and wash the fine cups with a caution bordering upon dread, for she had already broken several simply by squeezing them a bit too hard between her fingers.

Then at last, her day over, she could leave. But it was then probably, when she left the splendours and refinements of the Beaulieu house, that her own hut with its smoking lamp really appeared to her in all its clutter.

She would now set to work scrubbing and cleaning at home.

"But I've already washed," Winnie would protest, disheartened at having a daughter that nothing seemed to satisfy any more.

Next the lamp would be drawn to Elsa's side of the hut and she would settle down to her sewing and mending. She was possessed by a bewildering anxiety to make the cabin as gracious as the grand house of the policeman.

Her second and third months' wages went to buy a piece of linoleum to cover the unsightly floor and a pair of warm woollen blankets to replace the old animal skins that had become full of dust and germs.

Archie, who was beginning to be irritated by all these changes, ventured when he chanced to be home for a few days to speak his mind.

"What have you got against skins?" he asked Elsa.

"They're not washable," she said rather curtly and Archie did not know how to answer that.

Jimmy had just had his first birthday and was beginning to walk. From then on almost everything in the cabin was within his reach, to be carried to his mouth. All at once Elsa saw how many objects still lay about, despite all her efforts, that were not suitable or safe for children. There was only one solution; she bought a playpen like the one in which Madame Beaulieu imprisoned her youngest child.

Never before had such an interference with liberty been seen in an Eskimo family. Even Thaddeus, who always strictly minded his own business, suggested to Elsa that it was not right to restrict a little child who had just discovered the delight of being able to take himself wherever he wanted to go on his own two feet. He offered to keep an eye on the child from morning till evening — to the extent, if necessary, of not doing anything else — rather than endure the thought of his being a prisoner.

But Elsa had reached the point of no longer having too much confidence even in Thaddeus.

One would have thought the child already understood from what side help could be expected. Whenever his mother picked him up to put him in his pen — which completed the congestion in the cabin — he would give heart-rending shrieks and hold out his arms to Winnie or Thaddeus. Thaddeus would look away, showing his disapproval by a wounded silence. Winnie, however, felt no scruples against urging the child to rebel.

Things went on like this, more or less well, more or less badly. Then one day when Elsa had not been able to make her "dash" at her usual hour, she turned up later when no one was expecting her and found them all doing just as they pleased. The playpen, dismantled, had been put outside with the rubbish. His face smeared, Jimmy was messing about happily with some pups in a dish of evil-smelling fish. Seated on the floor, ostensibly to keep an eye on the child, Winnie was placidly smoking, watching the Koksoak flow by. It was a fine day, the door had been left half open, and Thaddeus could be seen leaning against a pile of empty oil drums, warming himself in the sun. Elsa's little brother was tossing stones in the air for the mere pleasure of doing so. Not for a long time probably had Elsa seen people so content with their lot. And it could not be denied, the truth stared her in the face: they were all much happier when she wasn't there. This cruel thought and her own tiredness doubtless overcame her at once. She made an attempt to catch her child, perhaps to wash him, but he burst into piercing screams, beat against her with his fists, and managed to escape. Suddenly Elsa, whom no one had ever seen crying before, dissolved in tears. How odd it was to see her, once so gay, weeping, arms hanging at her sides, in the centre of the cabin. No one knew what to do. Thaddeus turned his head away modestly and gazed into the distance towards the old eroded mountains as if to ask them what one should think of such a bitter sorrow caused by no one quite knew what.

Eventually Winnie seemed to understand and made a show of beginning to tidy up, promising changed ways starting tomorrow. It would kill her, she said, to take on everything there was to do here if she was to satisfy everyone, but she would try one more time. Her life was being used up, moreover, attempting to keep up with progress, a difficult master progress: did anyone know what it wanted and where it was leading people?

These words so angered Elsa that she stopped crying and began to stare at her mother. She saw then, as if for the first time in her life, a woman grown puffy from sleep and eating too much, always smoking or rolling a bit of food between her worn gums, the human being she was least anxious to resemble, even perhaps her worst enemy, an obstacle in any case on the road she was following towards a goal that constantly eluded her.

She tried once again to attract her child, holding out her arms, but he ran to snuggle into those of his grandmother. Winnie scarcely tried to conceal her triumph, her face so creased with happiness that it looked cracked — as cracked and fissured as one of the ancient stones of the tundra.

5

Fortunately for Elsa there was Sunday. That day never failed to renew her sense that one is not in this world only to perform one's daily tasks but must give space also to those musings that exalt and repose. Early in the morning, fresh and neat in her pink cotton dress, her black hair now cut short, she would set out for church with her beautifully dressed child in her arms.

Perhaps because he was white, or simply so that he could see far ahead, she had seldom carried him Eskimo-fashion on her back.

At the sight of them coming along the beach under the luminous sky, the child's hands clasped lazily around his mother's neck, she in all the charm of her wild timid beauty, one might have asked: Is this an image of reality? Or is it simply an illusion?

If he grew restless or whimpered during the sermon, she would rock him, whispering in his ear that he must listen well to God speaking.

The pastor, a man whom life had profoundly inured to the most tender as to the most cruel sights, still felt troubled by the sight of Elsa's child and did not quite know what to think of his presence among them. One Sunday during the sermon, he considered Elsa and the child and then, as if the impulse had just come to him, he spoke of human love, saying, "Nothing is less foreseeable. It is, in the fullest sense, the mysterious road by which we are led to the discovery of ourselves. One, begun in poor soil, can bring forth a rare flower. Another...."

At these words the congregation drifted into reverie. The humble brown faces, their eyes shining softly as if lit by distant lamps, all seemed lost in thought and they smiled and acquiesced with little nods of the head. What could be more true: in love nothing was foreseeable.

Then, as if they almost all perceived at the same moment where this thought would end, they turned their heads towards Elsa and smiled with what appeared to be warm approval.

She lowered her eyes shyly. It was perhaps for such instants that she considered it worthwhile to take all this trouble to make sure she and the child were always impeccable.

Nevertheless, she was growing visibly thinner and had come to wear that slightly harassed expression of her employer and other young white women who were always afraid they hadn't accomplished enough and kept setting themselves new and ever more incomprehensible goals. Doubtless to soothe the agitation of her nerves, she chewed gum incessantly even in church, though here more discreetly. Sunday after Sunday the pastor told himself he would call her aside and try to reason with her. But time passed without giving him an opportunity; or he would find suddenly that he dare not seize it, hindered by some indefinable confusion visible on Elsa's face for which he did not know the remedy.

The following summer the child still insisted upon being carried as soon as the ground became a little difficult or simply, at times, for the pleasure of riding at a good height and without fatigue.

They would pass along the rim of the summer sky, she a little curved, he piggyback at her graceful neck, and he would urge his mother along by motion and voice as if she were the steed and he the cavalier. She would obey, laughing, and sometimes even break into a trot to hear him join her laughter.

She was still in the service of Madame Beaulieu and had only her Sundays to go out with her child. First, unfailingly, she took him to church.

Afterwards they would go to a lonely corner of the beach, beyond the last of the Eskimo cabins at the point of a deeply indented cove where the Koksoak, more peaceful here, just skimmed some dark sleek rocks. High blocks, set in a semi-circle, cut off the peaceful enclosure. Perhaps it was the fact that she could distinguish the sound, faint though it was, of the scarcely moving water that led her to recognize the peace of this spot. Like everyone who tries to decipher his own thoughts, she needed solitude and could no longer find it on the common beach where all the families gathered on Sundays.

Jimmy also adored this place. When they left church, he already perched on Elsa's shoulders, he would get angry if he saw her take another direction and belabour her sides with his feet. But, soon perceiving that this was only a game to test him and that his mother was turning, he would change his mood abruptly and lean down cajolingly to stroke her face.

When they had finally passed the last cabin, that of Sarah, a very unsociable old woman who did not even come to her doorway to see them pass, and would not meet anyone henceforth but wandering dogs, Elsa would take off her good shoes and carry them hung by their laces from her neck.

Her shoulders already bent by life but her eyes released and raised to the bright sky, barefoot and in her Sunday clothes, with her child at her neck, she looked, as she followed the shore of the river and the distant parallel line of old round mountains, as if she had come from the beginning of the ages and would proceed, from stage to stage, to the end of time.

As soon as they reached their retreat, Jimmy would become excited and ask to get down from his mother's shoulders so he could run on ahead, though the pebbles of the beach were still very hard for his little feet. But in his impatience to arrive he no longer felt them. He would run stumblingly to a certain low rock at the water's edge, clamber up and then cast his eyes over the entire landscape as if he were trying, small as he was, to gather it all into a single gaze. At the same time he clasped his hands behind his back in the curious attitude of a man lost in contemplation. When he was away from the endless commotion, teasing, and pampering of the Eskimo village, there appeared in Jimmy another more gentle and dreamy child. Often, after he had contemplated water and sky, he would turn to his mother and give her a smile that seemed to be trying to tell her he was happy to be there with her.

At these moments she was delighted with him but disappointed too because no one but she knew him at his best.

She would spread out their lunch. When Jimmy had explored the surroundings and acquired an appetite, she would call him and tie a bib, which she had modelled after one at Madame Beaulieu's, around his neck.

Watching Elsa go like this from eccentricity to eccentricity, Winnie had come to the point of finding her behaviour quite inexplicable. She would hurry to the stoop to watch them depart and, no doubt vexed at being left all alone on a lovely day, pursue them with her sarcasms: "The girl must be crazy having a nice house, dishes, and a table, no, she must be clean out of her mind having all this comfort at home to go off and eat out of doors!"

Mother and child would seat themselves at either end of a flat rock and dine as neatly as possible, wiping their fingers frequently in the clean sand so close at hand. Jimmy always wore his Sunday suit, of a blue similar to his eyes, and his mother would caution him frequently not to dirty or damage it. Her life was being used up buying him clothes as costly and toys as charming as those possessed by the children of Madame Beaulieu. Yet, even alone with him here, with no other witness to all this elegance but the distant sky, she was as happy about it as at the performance of some obscure and marvellous duty.

After their meal she would wash him in the river and let him run about naked for a moment to dry in the sun. The crown of blond hair, now long and lightly curled, gave Jimmy a sort of halo like those of the little angels she had seen at the Catholic mission.

When he was tired or sometimes just in tenderness, he would come and sit beside her on the pile of pebbles facing the river. After studying his mother's attitude out of the corner of his eye, he would copy it as faithfully as he could, and remain there motionless, hands crossed over the stomach, eyes gazing far away.

Anyone chancing to pass by might have been astonished at the sight of these two creatures, so dissimilar and yet united by the same reverie. Later, during these hours of peace, she would try, no doubt out of gratitude towards life, to interest her little boy in what surrounded them. For instance, she would encourage him to recognize, in the shape of a stone, a bird with a long beak. And indeed, turned carefully in the light, the commonplace little grey stone did suddenly look somewhat like the stylized birds that came from Thaddeus' dreams. Jimmy would set to work delving in the sand with both hands, perhaps thinking he could dig up some of the beloved flying creatures of his Eskimo great-grandfather. Or she would use a piece of driftwood to try to show the tree from which it had come and indicate its beauty. But whatever she said, the bit of wood looked more like some unfortunate and strangely mutilated animal.

The child was far from understanding all this. But as his mother talked her eyes would shine even more than they ordinarily did. Perhaps he was entranced by the increased vivacity of those large dark eyes, for one day when she was talking with great animation he suddenly stretched out his hand as if to grasp them as he might two beautiful pebbles, their hues brightened by dampness.

Sometimes during those warm afternoons he would grow drowsy and would come and snuggle against Elsa's shoulder. She would draw him into her arms and rock him with a slow continuous motion. In the pale eyes that were on the point of closing, hazy and trustful, she would read a gentleness and sweetness that only showed in their entirety at such times. These were the only moments in her life when she still thought vaguely of the GI who had given her this child, wondering whether he too could be charming when he chose. She would look searchingly into the child's eyes for a moment, rather as if she were trying to find traces of someone. Then she would grow weary.

At length, despite the cool air from the river, mosquitoes would begin to seek them out. Patiently and incessantly, she would wave them away from the face of the sleeping child. Soon she, too, would feel heavy, and sleep would be hard to resist. And the images of her life would loosen and flee one before the other like the big white clouds of those tranquil days beside the Koksoak.

6

Another year slipped by before the pastor continued along the beach one Sunday after a visit to Sarah, who was now quite helpless, and came upon Elsa and her child, safe in their usual retreat.

As if at a half-open door, he seemed to wait for some gesture of welcome. Then, at a smile from Elsa, he advanced a few steps farther and sat down beside her on the riverbank. Absently, as almost everyone does the moment he has smooth flat stones within reach and water before him, he chose a few and tried to make them skip along the surface of the river. It had been a very long time since he had played this game and he felt astonishment first at his action and then a certain easement, as if there was still something in this old boyish gesture of men to lull the soul.

He slipped then almost without effort into sharing with Elsa the thought just come to him – that the soul probably gains by not taking itself too seriously.

Before them the child ran and leaped.

"Your Jimmy is growing," he noted.

"Today he's three years, five months and two days old," she informed him.

This precision, so little in the manner of the Eskimos, many of whom come to be not too sure of their ages — thus Sarah, for instance, had only an approximate idea of hers — brought a tender smile to his lips. Soon afterwards, however, they averted their eyes from one another, as if they had stumbled together against the same vague but still troubling memory. Did he for his part remember that he had felt at the very beginning almost an aversion to Jimmy's origin? And did she still at times recall the brief struggle in the agitated bushes? The pastor was in any case the only one who could rouse such hateful memories — conscience he called it. From time to time she had resented this. But it was as little in Elsa's nature to harbour resentment as it would have been for the river to flow back to its source. Soon, understanding that the pastor was looking at Jimmy with emotion, she too was all emotion, thanking him with her eyes for finding her child pleasing. On this face, contracted by so much pride, the pastor was able to read the extent of the tiredness and depletion that so rare a happiness exacted from the girl. Even her hands never stopped fluttering, unlike most Eskimo hands, which know how to lie still once work is done. As if the sight of those hands so uselessly busy was painful to him, the pastor looked away with a murmured reproach. One shouldn't take things so much to heart. One shouldn't wear oneself out at one's task.

Elsa raised her head in bewilderment mingled with a certain defiance: "But shouldn't we try all the time to be better?

"Certainly," said the pastor, "but with proportion, with patience."

He gazed with a pensive expression at the wide river, whose cold water gave off towards the middle of its expanse a fine trembling vapour laden with sun.

"Haven't you ever thought, Elsa, of getting married? To some nice boy of your own people who would take care of you and the child?"

He was startled by the sudden hardness that spread over Elsa's features.

"No," she said, "never."

"But why are you so set in your mind?"

In the delicate light of the afternoon she let her eyes follow the child — so quick, happy, and unique — and did not know what to say except that her soul was so preoccupied with him it had no room for anyone else. From morning till night since Jimmy was born, there had never been sufficient time for him.

"Precisely," said the pastor. "You live far too exclusively for him. So what will you do on the day he's taken from you?"

A swift reflex made her glance anxiously around her.

The pastor smiled.

"Not today. But some day, in the future."

The future! A word she found impenetrable. She tried, however, with her usual willingness, to understand, her face taut in concentration, but it was useless. Though her head was filled with impressions and fancies, she was still unable to picture to herself days that were not yet present. Even tomorow seemed far away and perhaps not quite certain. From the white men, it seemed to her, she had learned much that was excellent — for instance to get up early, to rush all day scarcely ever dawdling any more, to take up tasks by the clock and not by the inclination of the moment — but to follow them in this strange and constant concern about the future was beyond her. However, she felt uneasy all at once in the midst of her Sunday joy and began to fuss rather feverishly with the pebbles around her.

His face proferred to the mild wind that scattered his sparse hair, the pastor tried to make Elsa see something of what might await her in time to come. As he talked, he too played absently with fragments of polished rock. He enumerated the difficulties she would soon have to confront: a woman raising a child alone and he growing up and perhaps not always obeying her very readily.

At this she smiled faintly, reassured and a trifle condescending. She repeated the reply of her great-grandfather to anyone who urged him to prepare for the future: "Does a man who sets out on foot for a long journey across the tundra, quite sufficiently burdened from the first day, concern himself with what he will have to carry on the fifth or the tenth day when he is tired? To each day its good or its bad hunting."

"True," the pastor agreed. "But you, Elsa, are setting out more heavily burdened on the first day than your wise and sober ancestors ever did. See how many useless needs you've already created for yourself."

He cited the child's fine clothes, his red rubber ball, his soft leather boots set out of reach of the water on a pile of stones.

"I'm afraid," he said, "that you've embarked on that endless road of never quite enough possessions. Why do you dress your child so expensively and shower him with so many gifts?"

She considered him with astonishment and could only reply, from the depths of her being, "Why, because he's Jimmy."

He was for an instant disarmed by the essential truth of this cry from the heart.

"Yes," he said, "there will be only one Jimmy, just as there is and will be only one Elsa. Though we're as infinite in our number as grains of sand, we are all, each one of us, a being apart."

They mused on that, delighted for the instant simply to exist.

But soon the pastor's deeply compassionate spirit could not help being troubled and wishing to put Elsa on guard against the evils that might come.

"By raising your child apart," he said, "you run the risk of losing him even before it is natural for a child to leave his mother."

Elsa's small brown hands began to fidget again and her eyes to flit from side to side. But then what should she do?

"In the old days," he reproached her gently, "you were all carelessness, Elsa, now you're all care. Couldn't you again be a little as you were before? Couldn't you rear your child more simply, as you yourself were reared?"

"In filth!" she said indignantly. "Eating the guts of animals?"

"You're too quick to go to extremes," he said. "It's a question of rearing the boy with care but without the danger of his ever coming to be ashamed of you and Winnie and Thaddeus. Do you understand?"

Quite truthfully, she did not understand. For, after all her efforts to deserve praise, where was her fault? However, she could see that there was some contradiction between the pastor's words about her duty to the future and his advice to try to become carefree again. As he watched the movement of the lively eyes, which seemed to be telling themselves an amusing but rather sad story, the pastor thought he understood what she was thinking and, unexpectedly, agreed.

"I'm contradicting myself, it's true. But from the moment we begin to think, Elsa, we become involved in contradiction. You will see that yourself, later. We go forward from contradiction to contradiction with the feeling that it will probably resolve itself at last in certainty."

He rose, unfolding his gaunt, prematurely worn body. The almost bald head set on a long skinny neck suggested one of those odd birds you encounter in the farthest reaches of the tundra, which turn away their eyes at the passing of a human being. But he, far from turning away his eyes, tried to gather into his singular bird's glance everything that might chance to pass over this tragic desert.

7

The shadow that fell over Elsa's life that bright summer day beside the Koksoak would never again, perhaps, entirely dissipate. The pastor's lesson finally penetrated her mind and, when she had somewhat understood and her disquiet had grown, she went, prompt to extremes as she was, even further. She believed now that she must change everything about the way she was bringing up her child.

If she were not very careful, the white men would be quite capable one day or another of taking him away from her — the more so as he was one of their own and she had never felt that her own right to him was complete. This is what she gathered finally from the pastor's warning. And so it was that the resolution to flee everything that had once so attracted her took possession of Elsa's mind.

Actually, just as the ice forms in the autumn without the eye being able to catch the precise moment and there is now a solid bridge to cross, the resolution to depart had come to her unawares and one fine day appeared to her firm already.

To depart? For her that could have only one meaning — a return to old Fort Chimo.

This was not far, at least in distance, being just across the way, on the opposite shore of the Koksoak, though here, it was true, the river was a wide and turbulent estuary.

But once across that stretch of water, one was already in another world.

As she remembered it, the grass grew higher on that shore and the trees had more life. She discovered that she had more recollections than she had believed of the old Eskimo village of her childhood. Unprecise, however, they rose from far back in her memory like one of those haunting tunes we cannot quite manage to recognize.

She began to question her father, and particularly Thaddeus, since the latter was more disposed to speak of past times.

"What was it like over there, Grandfather, in the old days?"

The old man looked delighted that she should wish to appeal to his memories.

"It was blessed peace, my child. The Hudson's Bay Company boat touched our shores once a year with supplies, then it was over, we didn't see a soul – neither white men nor anyone else – till the next ship. I'm not speaking, of course, of our own white men, who spent their lives with us and shared ours so completely that the thought would never have occurred to anyone to consider them strangers. There was Tom McDougall, the representative of the Company, who spent twenty years of his life with us, and also our pastor, Elias Simpson, who stayed even longer."

As he invoked the past, Thaddeus continued, with very light strokes, to chip a little animal figure from one of their local stones. His words were in unison with his cautious and reflective movements. All his life he had been a man of conciliation and peace.

The child had approached to watch him work; nothing so captivated him as the emergence – step by step, you might call it – from the old hands, as wrinkled as sealskin, of delicate and subtle creatures.

"Grandfather, what are you making today?"

The old man laid his hand on the child's head.

"What would you like me to make?"

"Me," ordered Jimmy, to whom the idea had just occurred. "Do my portrait."

"You," said the old man.

He looked a little disconcerted and began to examine with an entirely new attention the face that was raised to his.

"It's just that I don't know whether I could. You have features and a nose of a sort I've never learned to make. And I'm a bit old to learn new things."

Jimmy danced and screamed, in one of those tantrums to which he had been inclined for some time, the moment he was crossed.

Old Thaddeus knew wonderfully well how to soothe a child.

"I'll learn your face in one of my dreams, that's always how I learn best. I'll wake up one morning all ready. In the meantime, if I find just the right little piece of stone, I'll make you a pair of otters at play."

Jimmy ran joyfully outside and began to rummage about in the piles of stones around the house.

Thaddeus resumed his account, delighted with the attention Elsa was giving him. Few people were interested nowadays in what he had stored up within himself about the years gone by. And soon this would all die along with himself and a few other old people.

"Today," he said, "there's a tendency to criticize and find fault with everything. It's said that the Company exploited us, that they plundered us. That's only one side of things. Actually the Company bought our furs while we bought little more from them than necessities. Flour, for instance. You would have to try to imagine a life without that godsend to understand what it meant to us from the very first day. Already we couldn't do without it."

He mused for a moment, a smile spreading slowly across his features.

"But I wonder whether the greatest blessing wasn't tea. This may not have been quite a necessity. You might even call it an extravagance. But how restorative it was on our journeys in the great cold! I can remember the first mouthful of hot, very sweet tea my mother tried to make me swallow when I was still a very young child. I didn't want to; I thought it was one of those nasty herbal potions used for fevers. My mother laughed, saying, 'Baby, you'll see when you taste it.' And in fact as soon as I'd tasted it I demanded more. For the first time in our lives a real warmth reached the depths of our bodies and souls, where we'd never been completely warmed before. I remember: we sat there in a circle around the igloo, passing the cup back and forth to one another, drinking and laughing in a sort of drunkenness."

Jimmy reappeared for an instant in the doorway, crying, "Why don't you get busy and make my otters?"

"Right away," Thaddeus promised and confided to Elsa, "What spoiled our life was that war between the peoples that live across the ocean. America joined in, no one quite knows why, and built a station among us, to listen to one wonders what. Our young men were hired to work on the USA machines. Then the Hudson's Bay also crossed the Koksoak. What could we do? Once the Company had moved? The history of the Eskimos and the history of the Company is one," the old man concluded. "For a long time it was the Company that went to the Eskimos. Now it may be the turn of the Eskimos to follow the store. How would I know!"

"However," said Elsa, "some of our people stayed in the old Chimo."

"Yes, that's true and at times I envy them. There's the old man called the Fox, the wildest and craftiest old fellow you could imagine. There's Ebeneezer and his wife. . . There's your uncle Ian . . . Nothing will ever get him over here – not the Hudson's Bay and not religion. Sometimes I tell myself I'd be glad to take his place – no one he need account to, a real falcon on the cliff. But no. On the cliff there's the wind and freedom but nothing else – no family, no children, no affection. That's the whole story of man in essence," Thaddeus concluded, "just that too difficult choice between life in the great outdoors, proud and self-sufficient, or with the others, in the cage."

One evening, as Thaddeus was singing the praises of the past, Winnie put in her word. She was sitting on the floor, back to the wall, a cigarette hanging from her lips, mending an old garment of her husband's. The smoke rose to her eyes, so blinding her that, head bent low over her work, she seemed to be sewing by touch.

"You and your fine life of the old times!" she grumbled. "You make me laugh! Do you know that in those dear good times two children out of three died in their first months? Just how many I lost myself I no longer quite remember. Go and look in the old cemetery on the other side. Read the epitaphs, what remains of them. The oldest person buried there is

David Koliuk, dead at fifty-two. I remember. We spoke of him as of an incredible phenomenon. No one knew to what they should attribute such a long life. Oh yes, let's talk about those good old times!"

She bit off a thread with one of her few remaining stumps of teeth and sighed rather bitterly. As much as indolent Winnie could hate anything, she hated those harsh times that were gone. She could not understand, after the long road they'd had to travel to reach a little more ease and comfort, how anyone should now despise or relinquish them. She also found it very odd that the defence of modern times should be left to her, who had always been accused of not keeping pace with progress.

She described it to them, however, in all its virtues and attractions another evening, sitting on the floor again mending the same garment. First there was so close at hand, as paramount attraction, the church service on Sundays. Next the movies at the Catholic mission. Then the splendid new supermarket with its shelves so crammed that she herself, who stopped by there continually, was still discovering something new at each visit – a different brand of soap or some canned food she hadn't tried. Finally, there was the arrival at the airfield on fine summer evenings of government officials and other important people, who had such comical dazed looks when they got out of the plane that the sight was quite the equal of any evening at the movies. How was that for entertainment? As well, when you were sick, there was the nurse who could find her way around all those rows of bottles and tubes and phials. How could anyone, advanced as they were on this side of the river, dream about the old Chimo, which was finally dying, anyway, in the midst of its tall grass and the plaintive sound of the wind?

Having spoken, Winnie beckoned furtively to Jimmy so she could slip a candy into his hand without Elsa's knowledge. She stuffed him with sweets from morning till night. There was no deceit or trickery to which she would not stoop provided he would give her in return a little caress or tell her he loved her better than his mother. When she had obtained this, she would thump herself on the thighs, her toothless mouth wide open in laughter, just like a witch delighted with her spells.

Actually, if there had been no one but Elsa, that crazy girl for whom one day there was not enough progress and too much the next, Winnie would have been glad to show her the door in person: All right, so you want your freedom; take it!

But there was the child. In Winnie's shrivelled and stunted old flesh there was now an entirely new feeling – adoration. Perhaps it was a source of as much torment as joy. But she would not have lost it for anything in the world.

From her young employer, however, came the most moving opposition to Elsa's plan and this she found hard to resist. So she let the summer slip by and with it the chance to leave that year.

Elizabeth Beaulieu was sinking into a deep melancholy that appeared incurable. Since the birth of her third child she seemed to have strayed into strange complicated corridors from which she could not manage to find the exit and where no one could reach her. She was there, outwardly quite close and yet isolated from everyone. She no longer entertained at tea. What would have been the use? She had no taste for anything. She stood almost perpetually, sad and thoughtful, at her window, unable to tear herself away from the fascination exerted upon her by the distant icy meeting of earth and sky. Winter had come early and the land, covered once more with snow, every hint of colour or warmth – rock and tufts of reddish lichen – now hidden, looked if possible more naked.

In the desert of sky and earth, the smoke from the cabins struggled against the cold with means so derisory they aroused only pity. Instead of the pleasant warmth and consolation of shelter, some vague distress seemed to mark those thin threads of smoke that rose here and there in the piercing air.

From time to time, no longer with much faith but simply out of willingness, she would go through the motions again of trying, as it was said, to attach herself to normal life. She would open one of the books in the pile friends had sent with the hope of distracting her. She would read a few lines. It was perhaps one of those novels dealing with what it is convenient to call the disgust or futility of life. Or she would read some reassuring passage; but everything in these books was so far from what was the truth here that the words could not reach her. She would choose a record: a light charming song would fill the snug little house in the depths of the infinite misery of the Arctic. Wounded by this gayety, she would stop the turntable. She would go back to her picture window, drawn despite herself by the immense naked land. The snow on sunless days was livid. With its long crests gathered by the wind, which one might have thought had been frozen in their moment of unfurling, like infinite waves, it formed a sort of petrified ocean.

"Elsa," she would call suddenly, as if in a cry for help.

"Yes, madame."

Elizabeth would look at her little Eskimo maid, from whom she was obliged to expect assistance.

"I'm so lonely, if you just knew how lonely I am, Elsa!"

Loneliness – that in itself Elsa was now able to understand. Yet why should this young lady, who was so surrounded by everything that was beautiful and happy, be lonely?

Elizabeth was longing for busy streets, teeming shops, the comforting stir and movement of cities. It was quite useless to try to get Elsa to imagine such things.

"Sit down," she would ask her as a favour. "Talk to me."

Sit down, talk! Elsa did not willingly submit. Things went almost well with her as long as she ran, rushed about and polished. But if she stopped and allowed herself a moment's reflection, she too was overwhelmed by a confused aspiration towards another sort of life, half understood and yet calling her incessantly.

She would finally sit on the very edge of one of the soft chairs. She would fold her hands and raise her beautiful dark eyes, full of attention, to Elizabeth.

"Tell me something, anything, Elsa."

Elsa would glance at the piles of books as if to say: Shouldn't you ask them to tell you something?

"No, you," Elizabeth would beg. "Talk to me a bit about your life. What was it like – the life you Eskimos lived in the old days? Do you remember?"

Elsa would cling to the arms of the too soft chair that always gave her the impression she was about to fall over backwards. The life of the old days? She raised her eyes, stretching her memories as one stretches one's whole body to reach a high object barely within reach of the hand, and suddenly the lassitude in her big eyes gave place to a warm glow.

"It seems to me," she said, "that in those days we were often cold and hungry in the igloo. But when we weren't either cold or hungry, then, it seems to me, we laughed."

"Ah!" said Elizabeth, immediately less tense. "But about what, Elsa? What could you have laughed at?"

Elsa shrugged. She did not know. She had forgotten or might never have known. About nothing perhaps. All she could say was that she thought she remembered hearing more laughter when she was a child than there was now.

She would be permitted finally as a great favour to go and finish the housework or take the children, well wrapped-up, for a walk.

But she could no longer defend herself against the incomprehensible pain of her young employer. Why did Madame Beaulieu suffer so much? She had everything: beautiful children, an expensive house with the rock as a pedestal from which to look out over the whole country, a soft warm interior, woollen carpets, pictures on the wall, and above all a loving husband who enquired with solicitude each evening when he came home, "Don't you feel a little better tonight, my darling?" The most pampered, best-loved creature in Fort Chimo was nevertheless ailing and sad. This sorrow without apparent cause troubled Elsa more than some ordinary sorrow, such as might have befallen herself or her mother, for instance. The sorrow of the whites must be a sign that no one could escape. Vaguely it occurred to her at times that progress might be the cause. She would feel afraid of this terrifying force that was perhaps beyond all human endurance. It was for her own sake now as much as to save Jimmy that she thought continually about fleeing to the other side of the Koksoak.

But month after month Elizabeth implored her to stay a little longer.

"At least till the snow melts."

Then, "At least till the birds return."

Finally one afternoon, after practising for a long time behind the door, Elsa came in to announce in a single breath that she couldn't wait any longer and must leave at once.

As if Madame Beaulieu had hoped right till that moment that the separation would not take place, she burst into harsh sobs.

"You too are forsaking me!"

This violent grief touched Elsa as she had never been touched before by the grief of any of the whites. But at the same time she felt proud, uplifted, because for once in her life she had the sense in the presence of a white person that she was simply one human being beside another.

"Elsa has to go," she said of herself as of someone over whom she did not possess all powers. She must, it was true, but this would not be forsaking one who had now become her friend for life.

TWO

8

Summer had clothed the dwarf trees somewhat sketch-
ily in a timorous foliage, whose rustling was only
barely audible. Back from the golden beaches of the
Carolinas and Florida, terns stood in a single motionless row beside the Koksoak, gazing at it for hours as if
they had long been impatient for another glimpse of
this cold and magnificent river of the north. At last
everything was ready for the departure of Elsa and
the child. They were seen off by Thaddeus, Winnifred,
several of their neighbours, and some dogs.

Archibald was to take them across the river in his
mended boat. After several trial turns, the motor
caught. The boat was shuddering already, for even
near its shores the river is impetuous. Elsa raised her
eyes and saw that her mother, instead of lamenting
or prophesying disaster, was standing silent and
dispirited beside the others on the beach. Her
face looked shrunken. In this wretched life Jimmy had
been a rare gift – "unbelievable" as she herself called
it. And now in the excitement of leaving, he did not
even think of speaking to his grandmother. At this
moment the old woman was quite incapable of rous-
ing any resentment in Elsa. She gave Jimmy a little
shake.

"Say at least good-bye to Granny."

He waved and shouted so joyfully it was almost offensive, "Good-bye, Granny Winnie."

She gazed at him with devotion.

The boat shot forward and, from the shore, was soon only a speck on the turbulent water. Jimmy beamed, entranced by the speed, the harsh caress of the air, and the freedom of the skiff. They swept on smoothly for a moment and then, without warning, the motor stalled. Immediately they began to drift, flung about by the swell, which they could hear pounding against the flat bottom of the boat. In addition, they were being dragged by the ebbing tide. Elsa seized the oars and pulled vigorously, trying to hold the boat. Archibald poured in more gasoline and primed the motor. With this simple breakdown the Koksoak had become a dangerous river once more and all the difficulties of the past were back again.

Finally the motor caught after they had been carried quite some distance. There was a second breakdown a little later. So it was late afternoon when they beached in an absolutely deserted sandy cove. Once the motor was turned off, the silence seemed to come to them unbroken from the beginning of time. The child raised his head, surprised, then at once delighted. Elsa had already observed that Jimmy was unusually sensitive to nature in its savage state.

Archibald looked completely at a loss. The moment he was without the noise of machines, which he had loved from the beginning as a reassuring pulsation from the world outside, anxiety and unease would mark his broad, open face. It was true, now that their ears had become attuned to it, they could hear the faint lapping of the water as it came to quench itself in the sand. Perhaps this desolate place seemed even more so since only a few years before it had been the liveliest town in the region. It was still there beyond the grey rocks – the wooden chapel, the Hudson's Bay post with its outbuildings, and about ten houses but, apart from a few of these that were still faintly alive, it was all dead and more melancholy to the eye than the desert, with boarded-up windows and doors nailed shut.

As for that old fool of an Ian, he lived even farther away, alone, at the tip of the nearest rocky point a good mile from here, beside a stretch of such rough water that Archibald had not wanted to risk landing there.

He began to unload Elsa's effects – the rolled-up tent, a sleeping-bag, a bundle of provisions, and the carbine he had given her.

He offered to carry them all over to the neighbourhood of Ian's cabin, but Elsa thought it would be better for her to present herself without baggage and first make sure of her welcome. Her belongings would be quite safe where they were for a day or two.

Just as she thought best, said Archibald. If her welcome left anything to be desired, she need only light a fire here tonight as a signal, and he would come and fetch her.

He got back into his boat. He in no way approved of this venture. But to each his freedom. To him, just touching this inhospitable shore where he had suffered such cruel deprivation was enough to arouse a superstitious fear. The sooner he left it, the better. He had only one thought: to get back as soon as possible to "town."

"Good-bye and good luck, Elsa."

The skiff faded into the distance. Elsa took Jimmy by the hand. The lightest of their possessions on their backs, they climbed up the grey rocks. Grasses grew here and there in hollows and cracks. They moved in an enveloping silence, which was vaguely reminiscent, like a dream, of long ago events. Elsa loved that silence. Suddenly it swelled with a gentle, prolonged, rather plaintive sound. They reached the summit of the second rocky fold and now Elsa discovered the source of that curious sound. Before them, in another undulation of the rock in a sort of little meadow, lay the old cemetery. At its entrance stood two sentinel trees; there were others here and there among the graves. It was these trees, with a light wind in their foliage, that gave forth the moving rustle.

She listened with pleasure. People had spoken so much evil of old Fort Chimo. Why had they not also told her of its trees?

She took a few steps more, listening to their sighing, and wondered how they had grown so tall.

Sheltered in this shallow dip in the ground, they had perhaps pushed their roots a little more deeply than is usually possible here before they struck the permafrost. But that alone was not enough to explain their good health. There must also have been someone who took good care of them – probably the first white man who lived in this region.

Elsa pictured him finding a little more earth here and there, protecting the roots in winter with lichen and moss, fetching water in summer from the river – all this, perhaps, less for the trees in themselves than as a memorial to someone dead, so that today they were a moving testament to love.

She took Jimmy's hand and led him into the cemetery. As they drew closer, the rustling of the little trees seemed to become more guarded as does the murmuring of people speaking in secret when someone approaches.

The graves were marked by little wooden crosses, which had stood the rigours of the climate fairly well though the inscriptions were beginning to fade.

"We came just in time," said Elsa mysteriously.

She stopped here and there, struggling to decipher the few words that remained. On this point at least Winnie had told the truth: life seemed to have been brief here, for the whites as well as for the Eskimos. She was standing before the plot of a family called Black from Scotland. A whole series of wooden crosses told the pitiful story: David, beloved son of Emily and George Black, raised in the love of his parents to the age of eleven months; Sarah, his sister, departed at the age of seven months and twelve days; Eleanor, deceased at three years. Then finally Emily herself, called to a better world at the age of thirty-two.

Was it because of Emily Black that the trees of the cemetery had so much vitality? The sadness of this unknown life reached Elsa from far in the past.

But if the little cemetery spoke of the cruel life of former days, it also spoke, as do few places in the world, of brotherly accord. Here Eskimos and whites lay side by side, under the same sort of crosses, in similar plots enclosed by slender picket fences, hand-carved into an artless design of lace and flowers. The whites had provided the humble pine – a rare material here – and the Eskimos the artist whose hand had perhaps trembled as he broached the precious substance.

Pensively Elsa continued her inspection. Suddenly on a tottering cross among the grasses, she made out a barely decipherable name.

"Jimmy," she called eagerly. "Come quickly. Here lies your great-grandmother. I have heard of her. She was called Jessica."

"Where?" Jimmy demanded, casting a swift and astonished glance around him. "Where she is my great-grandmother Jessica?"

Elsa smiled to see him search, as if for a living person, for this woman who had died so long ago, though she too when very young. But soon the smile left her face. What reminder of the brutal past had finally come to her? For several moments the cemetery had been in shadow. Under the increasingly overcast sky it had a derelict look.

"Come," she said, drawing Jimmy towards the gate. "Let's hurry so we'll be at Uncle Ian's by daylight."

The child may have remembered the discussions between Winnie and his mother and all that had been said about the prickly nature of Uncle Ian. He pressed against his mother.

"Will Uncle Ian refuse to let us in?"

She pretended to be amused at this and stooped to arrange his curls.

"No, no. Uncle Ian will say, 'Who is this beautiful little boy who has come to see me?'"

This, however, was the thing she was least sure of at present. As she started up another fold of the bleak rocks, she seemed to have assumed the gait of the women of her race in the old days when they were almost always on the move.

9

As they came out of a narrow pass, they saw Ian, seated on a low rock near his flimsy cabin, repairing the harness of one of his dogs, huskies of good stock, all five of whom were lying a short distance away, their muzzles flat against the ground.

Ian had certainly seen them — and how could he not be astonished at the sudden appearance in this place of a woman with a very young child? — yet, face bowed over his work, he went on with it as if nothing had happened.

It was a grim spot, almost heartbreaking in its wildness. Close to the cabin door the river, as broad here as an arm of the sea and as tempestuous, had been beating for centuries against the rocky shore, gashing it deeply and moulding it into weird shapes. Behind the hut, on a hummock of drab grey rock, stood a single brownish spruce. Its three remaining skeletal branches clawed the air with a ceaseless melancholy sound. Elsa hesitated for a moment before she took a few more steps towards Uncle Ian, who was still behaving as if he had not noticed them. It was clear that he was not going to be first to speak. Then, squeezing Jimmy's hand, she spoke with a sort of nervous vivacity, trying to sound playful.

"Hello, Uncle Ian. We bring you greetings from the family and from Fort Chimo."

The heavy eyebrows, as rough and tangled as handfuls of reindeer moss, drew together in a frown.

"Fort Chimo? Where's that? There's only one Fort Chimo and it's here. And besides who are you to call me Uncle?"

"Winnifred and Archibald's Elsa, Uncle Ian."

"Ah good . . . ! And him?" he asked, indicating Jimmy with his chin. "You're not going to tell me he's also of Archibald's seed."

She felt her child's hand tremble in hers and plucked up courage to say, "You know very well it's my little boy Jimmy."

At last Uncle Ian raised his eyes and enfolded the child in a single impassive glance.

"In the old days," he said, gazing towards the sea in the distance, "the white men and the Eskimos lived in harmony without mixing their blood."

"What's done is done," she said. "What's the use of going on talking about it all the time?"

He studied her in silence, eyes all attention now in the stone face.

"Just what is it that you want of me?"

"For you to keep us . . . a few days . . . a little while . . . perhaps for always, Uncle Ian . . . I'd like to try to learn the old ways. . . ."

"Come in," he said at last. "For the rest, we'll see."

Actually the invitation to come in had been made, or in any case was interpreted, symbolically. Elsa lived to one side in her tent, which was perfumed by the scent of the tide and of the intrepid spruce. She was a thousand times better there than in Ian's malodorous cabin, which she had not yet been permitted to clean though her desire to do so increased every day. Whenever he went hunting or fishing she took the liberty of doing a little scrubbing, without disarranging anything too much. She washed his clothes and mended them with beautifully tiny, even stitches.

He either did not notice or did not want to notice.

Almost every day he left some game or fish at the entrance of the tent. She prepared it and carried a portion to the stoop next door. This behaviour became intolerable to her and one day she sent Jimmy over with Uncle Ian's meal. He was not rebuffed, so she continued.

On Ian's doorstep the little boy would stop and let his eyes grow accustomed to the dimness, for at all times, even with the door open, the cabin was smoky and as dark as a cavern. Soon he would begin to make out an incalculable number of objects piled up here and there. At the very back he would finally distinguish the strange and inscrutable face of his great-uncle. Oddly, in this primitive and badly kept dwelling, there was a horsehair chair, now half devoured by the dogs, and in this Ian usually sat.

The child would approach. Uncle Ian neither encouraged nor repulsed him. The immobile face fascinated the little boy. One day he dared go very close to scrutinize it at his leisure. Ian did not stir under the attentive examination of those eyes, which were as bright in that murkiness as the light from a bit of sky at the entrance to a grotto.

"You have the blackest face I've ever seen," Jimmy concluded at last. "You're much blacker even than Archibald."

"Archibald," said Uncle Ian disdainfully, "is a slave living in captivity."

No doubt startled that Uncle Ian had finally spoken to him, the child found nothing more to say for a long moment. He continued to study in silence the eyes that avoided his own, looking above and past him, and said suddenly in astonishment, "You're angry. You're always angry!"

Ian lowered his gaze then as he complimented the perspicacious child.

"Yes," he admitted, "I'm angry."

Jimmy raced over to confide joyfully to his mother that Uncle Ian had said he was angry all the time.

"But not with us. Not with you," she assured him.

Nevertheless, day after day Ian continued to pass the tent without even turning his head in that direction. One evening he closed the ramshackle door of his hut, which on a summer night when there was neither wind nor many mosquitoes, was the height of incivility. But this was seemingly only a test, for early the next morning he stopped before the tent. Gazing into the vast expanse of moving water, he offered his invitation in a peremptory tone.

"I'm taking the little fellow fishing today if he has the heart for it."

It was the mother's courage that faltered. She knew Ian's fragile craft and the dangerous narrows that must be crossed to reach the current of the river; she also knew the unruly nature of her little boy and his inability to be still for very long. She drew back the flap of the tent and considered the water in the distance: it seemed calm today but even a slight wind would make it choppy. She sensed that she was being examined searchingly by the slit eyes of her uncle. At last she nodded her head in consent.

She watched them go off together between the rocks towards the shelter Ian had rigged up for his kayak ten minutes walk away. As they reached a small elevation and were outlined against the sky, she saw Jimmy slip his hand into that of the man, which did not withdraw. They moved, now joined to one another, against the infinite horizon, then descended the slope on the other side and disappeared from her sight.

All day the anxiety that constricted her heart did not loosen. But she refused to let herself try to follow the kayak's passage across the dangerous narrows from a raised point of ground or, later, go to see whether they were visible yet in the open sea. She forced herself relentlessly to sew, to gather twigs, and finally to prepare some bannock dough and set it to cook on a rock she had heated in advance. The hard unleavened bread began to give off a pleasant odour.

Towards the close of the afternoon, her ear, straining to hear the slightest sound, caught and recognized in the distance Jimmy's small excited voice. Soon she realized that he was talking incessantly as he always did when he was intensely happy and had a willing listener close at hand.

Finally the pair appeared on a ridge. Ian was carrying on his shoulder a good supply of fish threaded on a pole, as was Jimmy also, on a smaller pole. Dead-tired as he must be, he lengthened his steps to keep up with Ian's. He held his face turned up to his uncle's, chattering in a clear musical voice that the silence seemed to listen to with astonishment.

Ian assented with little bobs of the head.

Elsa went into the tent, sat down on the ground, and smiled broadly. For the first time in ages she felt unperturbed. It seemed to her that she had just turned the last page of an interesting but somewhat complicated book and was beginning another. The pastor was right: it was thus they must try to live.

10

In the autumn she moved into the hut, making do at night with the sleeping-bag in a corner; for greater warmth, she covered it with furs. With Ian's guidance and help — the practice was beginning to be lost in the new Fort Chimo — she made Jimmy a suit of caribou and also boots for the winter. He was wild with joy and did not want to take them off, even to sleep. Sometimes when she looked at him, Elsa observed that he was less clean and neat than before. But he was also less inclined to have temper-tantrums at every turn.

They had, you might say, no neighbours. Almost all the remaining inhabitants of Fort Chimo lived near the abandoned store and chapel, as if hoping for a resurrection of the happy village of former days, and they were for the most part elderly taciturn people and little inclined to sociability. Jimmy had no young companions but Ian's dogs, and between himself and them there grew up an attachment that was more moving from day to day.

One fine morning after the snow came he found at the cabin-door a small sleigh Ian had made just for him. He learned to drive it in the Eskimo fashion, standing behind, feet firmly planted on the runners, urging on his favourite dogs, Yappy and Stormy, with shouts. He used to go out alone on pretended journeys.

In the intense cold, half hidden in the fur hood, his face was radiant.

Yet living so simply still required that they never be idle. Ian spent his days hunting and making the round of his traps. Elsa scoured the beach tirelessly, in search of the bits of wood that the sea consented at times to send their way. One day she brought back a beam that had probably come from some distant shipwreck. Chopped in small pieces and eked out for as long as possible, this fragment of a dead ship participated in many pleasant evenings of reminiscences and stories around the fire. Elsa shared this thought with Ian, who shrugged. He was not given to such fancies.

On the other hand, despite the resentment that events of the last years had roused in him against the white men and their example, he had remained faithful to the Word.

Since the Reverend Hugh Paterson, after cruel hesitation, had finally decided to follow the bulk of his flock, who had already emigrated to the new Fort Chimo, Ian had not attended service. But in his own way he was steadfast in his observance of Sunday. On that day he washed and more or less untangled his hair with his fingers. He would take his place in his chair and, at the hour when the wind sometimes brought the sound of the bells of the new church, he would open his book of Bible stories. He would look at the pictures and examine pages here and there, trying to remember the texts their pastor, whose voice he could still hear in his memory, used to read in the old days.

There were other books in the hut. Their presence, in the dust under the benches, was a story in itself. The George Black of the cemetery had been a great reader and one day a whole trunk of books had come for him from Scotland. Before his death, concerned about his books or merely wanting to give them to someone who would be able to appreciate them a little, he had summoned Ian's father and asked him, "Will you take them?"

To accept books was a great responsibility, in view of the space they took up and the frequent moves of those days. Ian recalled the hesitation of his father, though he was fond of books and united by a bond of gratitude to the Black family from whom he and his relatives had learned to read a little during their summers spent near the Hudson's Bay post. He agreed that between journeys he would give a glance at the books, which would be left in some safe place. The obligation had fallen to Ian in his turn. He had often, he said, been tempted to burn the lot when fuel was scarce. But he could never bring himself to do it, prevented by his feeling that a sort of life persisted in these pages. Now Elsa could read them if she liked, when there was nothing better to do – in the evenings, for instance, or on stormy days.

They had managed to find space for a wooden crate to serve as table and around this they used to gather. The lamp hung from the ceiling. Its glow caught the brightness of their eyes while leaving the roughness of the cabin in shadow. The damp wood burned slowly. From time to time a drop of water chased by the fire exploded with the hissing of an angry little animal. Elsa undertook to read *Ivanhoe* aloud. Ian, who believed he knew the story, having heard it read before, was surprised to follow it with new interest, either because he had listened carelessly the first time or because now, as he said half seriously, Elsa was adding bits here and there.

She soon felt a passion for these old dog-eared books such as she had felt in her youth for the movies — an even stronger passion, for the source of delight was now close and certain, truer too, perhaps, and she herself better able to draw from it. She was inconsolable when she found gaps, sometimes three or four pages torn from the book.

According to Ian, she shouldn't worry too much about this; it did not prevent their understanding the story and, after all, it was sufficiently wonderful that the books had reached them, whatever their condition.

On the other hand she was moved by the slightest sign of the passing of another reader: a sentence underscored or notes in the margin in a cramped script that she always stopped to decipher. She would feel at such times, as one does on the tundra at the sight of some displaced stones or trodden reindeer moss, that a human being had just crossed the infinite barren land and with a little luck one might still perceive in the distance his moving silhouette.

One evening when she had paused in her reading for a moment to let it reverberate within herself, she caught, in the glow of the lamp, Jimmy's excited look. His reaction was that of all children who like to hear stories. He wanted more, always more. Elsa decided to teach him to read, so that he too would know the crossroads and byways that books are, and be able to enjoy them.

Every evening now the raw wooden crate was cleared, as once the bath-table had been, especially for Jimmy, and the lamp drawn close. He learned to mark his name with a chisel on soft stone – Jimmy Kumachuk – and liked to see it written out at length, passing the tip of his tongue over his lips in satisfaction.

But Elsa was sad because he had nothing to write on but stone. She was anxious to have paper and pencils for him.

Paper! Paper!

Ian at first was stubborn.

"Today paper. Tomorrow what? Besides, stone is better."

"You can't send it through the mail as a letter," said Elsa.

"Has anyone even tried?" Ian retorted.

However, he finally became quite agreeable to Elsa's demands, and allowed the promise to be drawn from him that when he crossed the river to make the necessary purchases he would bring back paper – but only if he found any that was thick enough, because if he came back with sheets through which you could see daylight, they might as well do without.

"And pencils," Elsa added.

Ian made a surly reply: it went without saying that for paper you needed pencils.

At last the ice on the Koksoak was solid enough to cross. Ian harnessed the dogs and, his fringe icy, enveloped in the steam of his own breath, he informed Elsa that he was going to the new Fort Chimo to sell his dressed furs and get his year's supplies. Would she like to come? Or would she not just as soon stay?

She shook her head gently, understanding that he was afraid that if he took them there she might hesitate to return.

With all Ian brought back – paper, pencils, food and news—there were provisions enough for the whole winter. First, news of the family. They were well, said Ian, except that Winnie had to go and get injections in the thigh twice a week from the government. She said she was suffering from a curious sickness he had never heard of before and whose name he had forgotten. In any case, her blood was changing to sugar, which was no cause for astonishment when you remembered that Winnie had eaten sugar by the handfuls all her life. This had done her no good; in spite of or because of all this sugar, she was melting away. As for Archie, he had been hired by Nordair at Frobisher Bay to patch up broken planes.

So much for news of the family. As for news of the world, it was not good, not good at all.

Ian removed his mukluks, sat down on the floor with his back against the wall and cast a look of unhabitual friendliness upon the domestic objects. On the stove steamed the little teapot, now terribly blackened with age, which had accompanied him on most of the journeys of his life.

Elsa poured him a mug of the very strong tea he liked and urged him on gently for, having talked much more than he usually did, he seemed weary already.

"So what is the news of the world?"

He said it was foolish beyond belief. The same little soldiers they'd seen freezing here at the time of the second world war were perhaps getting themselves soaking wet on the other side of the world, in Korea where the United States had another squabble on its hands.

He had gone the previous night to the pastor's, he said, to get an explanation of the war and the conduct of the nations. The most expensive thing at the present moment was defence. The countries kept on inventing weapons — one day one, the next day another.

His mug in his hand, knees drawn up, he paused in sombre reflection.

"We are almost the last men who do not know war. Because we are too poor and far from the invasion routes. . . ."

He gave a sort of strange and bitter laugh, he who laughed so seldom.

"That's what I thought till yesterday. I was mistaken. The invasion routes now pass by the North Pole."

"The routes! By the Pole!"

"When I was a child," Ian told her, "we often heard about white men who were racing to be first to plant their flags at the Pole. Now they go over it or under it with their bombs. As for poverty. . . ."

His eyes dulled, heavy with melancholy.

"It seems that we are not at all poor. Our icy seas and our frozen subsoil contain treasures, our pastor says, and it won't be long before we see strangers arriving to dig and delve and set everything topsy turvy. . ."

He lowered his glance to Jimmy who stood close to him listening, his eyes big with wonder. He laid his broad palm on the child's head.

"Ah poor us," he concluded in a sort of wish, "may God save us from treasures!"

Later the fact of having paper and pencils prompted Elsa to write some letters. She had been shown how at school: where to put the date, her own address and that of her correspondent. "Suppose," said the teacher, "that someone dear to you was far away or you yourself were far away and you wanted to share your news with that person. . . ." Elsa had never been able to suppose any such thing and yet it was true: she now had people to write to. So she wrote as she used to at school, in play, "Dear mother," and then for a long time had trouble knowing how to proceed. Finally she thought of saying she was distressed to hear that Winnie was sick from sugar. She hoped sincerely that she'd eat less of it in future.

However, her long letter of the winter, at which she worked evening after evening in the poor light, was intended for Madame Beaulieu — but would she ever manage to finish it?

"Dear little madame of Canada," she had begun valiantly, only to remain there, quite at a loss.

The despondency of the young woman, though she was as pampered as anyone could be, had never, to tell the truth, left her memory or ceased to be a source of confusion to her. She rewrote twenty times the sentence in which she told her not to be too sorrowful as she stood at her picture window watching the sun set; if it went down red, this was in any case a sign of fine weather the next day. She decided that it was perhaps not for her to give advice to someone whose position was incomparably higher than her own.

On the other hand, to show herself as happy and content with her lot to someone who was not might seem heartless. She tried out several ways before it occurred to her that she should present herself to Madame Beaulieu as not having too easy an existence herself. She described the difficulties of her life: the fire that was slow to catch and did not give very much heat, since the wood was still damp from the sea — but what luck to find that heavy beam — then the food that was of necessity the same day after day. However, Jimmy was thriving on this regime and had lovely pink cheeks and a much better disposition now.

When she had written all this, she realized that she had not managed to sound very pitiable. But she was not prepared to go on indefinitely crossing out everything she wrote.

Besides, she was weary of writing. She would never have believed the effort took so much out of one. To follow her own thoughts as she might follow the racing of the clouds or, idly, the current of the water was one thing; to run after them, track them down and enclose them in words was quite another. In the very middle of a sentence she stopped, not knowing how to get out of it, and concluded without more ado, signing herself, now and forever, "a friend," Elsa.

11

In this remote part of the world, so long frozen,
summer was of unhoped-for sweetness. Once again
the wind drew from the grasses between the wooden
crosses a gentle rustling that seemed to link together
all that had been suffered here by white men and
Eskimos alike. It was as if the brief compassionate
season found its fullest expression in this little cemetery, which was warm still with the attachment of the
living to the dead.

As she passed in her search for edible berries, Elsa
loved to go in and sit on a stone that was half covered
with wild grass. A sense of numerous presences, invisible but close, would gradually steal over her. She
would feel besieged by confidences from lives that
had had no one to talk to. Soon a stooped and tottering
figure would appear. This was Inez, the oldest inhabitant at present of the little dying community of old
Fort Chimo. She was toothless and almost deaf, with
filmy eyes, but the ancient bobbing head was brim-
ming with memories. She would search among the
graves for that of her mother, the first Eskimo woman
to be buried here. Soon afterwards she had been joined by the first white woman to die in this place — of
want also, Inez said. One did not die of anything
else in those days. Elsa would help her find the two
graves. Inez remembered even harsher times when

they used to bury the dead in the infinite tundra, under heaped-up pebbles or rocks to protect them at least for a little while from wolves.

It was a miracle life had even been able to continue, since so many people died so young at that time.

"Before they'd learned their names," said Inez. "Yes, my child, and sometimes even before they'd been given a name." The old head began to shake. "Now we go on wandering through life long after we've stopped being good for anything. Which is worse," she asked in a querulous small voice, "to die too soon or to live too long?"

She strained her ears suddenly towards the little trees, which a slight wind was stirring.

"Is there someone rummaging about over there?"

"No, Grandmother," said Elsa. "It's just the trees."

"The little trees!" sighed Inez. "I saw them born."

She hunched within her ancient black fringed shawl, come here in who knew what trunk of fine goods from Scotland.

"Who are you?" she asked at each of her meetings with Elsa.

Elsa would patiently tell her again.

One day when Jimmy was there, Inez turned towards him eyes that were blurred with cataracts, struggling to make out something of the childish face.

"Is this child yours? Where did you get him?"

"From an American soldier," said Elsa simply, Inez's long experience of life giving her confidence. "He had come up here to train in the cold but he's probably in Korea now."

"Yes," said Inez, "I see. Well, in Korea too, as you say, he must have left a child. It will perhaps all be settled in that way."

"What will, Grandmother?"

"Life," said Inez.

She reflected, her face, because of her great age, always tilted now towards the ground.

"If soldiers are continually being sent far from their homes, they're bound to get lonely and will make children to leave behind them. Thanks to war and the mixture of blood, the human race will perhaps finally be born. We had a pastor in the old days," she continued, "who spoke only of that — a single family uniting all the nations."

She searched with difficulty far back among her memories.

"We didn't understand much of what he said, since there weren't any other peoples for us to be friends with. But perhaps that's also why we've lived in peace. Nowadays you seem to hear of nothing but war. But just what is war actually? Have you ever seen it?"

"No," said Elsa with regret.

"Ah, you haven't either. Well, no matter. That's perhaps better after all."

She managed to raise her head a little to peer at the luminous sky.

"It's a lovely day," she said. "And if it weren't for the pension from the government I wouldn't even be in this world. It's curious, all that. The government, which has never seen us, gives us enough to live on when we're no longer good for anything or anybody. That isn't the way to make death easier. To leave when you would have enough to live forever — that's hard. Yet I'd also like to go. Ah," she said. "I no longer understand anything. It's become too difficult."

And she hobbled away, mumbling that she would be better off now in her place in the cemetery with the people of the old days.

With October the frost touched the lichens at night just enough to make them take on their waning colours. The ancient rocks they clothed looked like small hanging gardens brilliant with flowers.

One day when Elsa was standing with Jimmy on the summit of one of those rocks overlooking the Koksoak, they saw a boat leave the opposite shore seemingly headed their way. Against the background of water traversed by choppy little waves, it could not for some time be identified. Finally, Elsa thought she recognized the police craft. Her heart, so calm the instant before, fluttered.

Perhaps she and her people had never become quite used to the presence among them of the police – a reminder of the endless increase of constraints. However, Elsa soon managed to reassure herself; none of the old people on this side of the river could have committed an offense grave enough to draw reprimand from the authorities.

Soon, moreover, she remembered that in their policeman there were two distinct persons — the one certainly whose duty it was to enforce the law but also the kind and sympathetic husband of her dear Madame Beaulieu.

Leaping from level to level, she ran to meet the latter.

Roch Beaulieu never set foot in this place without also being struck by that distant rustling. But he did not know of its source in the little cemetery and attributed his happiness at hearing this pleasing unknown sound to his own state of mind, which was suddenly freer.

For it seemed to him too that there was peace on this shore. Because he had never yet had to come to arrest anyone? Possibly, though he did not very often have to deal severely on the other side.

Jimmy was first at the foot of the cliff and greeted him excitedly, the only white man he had seen for a long time.

Soon afterwards came Elsa, smiling and motioning towards the rock from which she had just descended as she might have indicated a bench or corner of her own house. They climbed up and seated themselves on the crest and there, for a few minutes, they watched the Koksoak flowing and let its soothing voice enter their spirits.

Finally, when Jimmy had withdrawn a short distance, the two adults slipped, without much urgency, into conversation.

How was Madame Beaulieu now? Elsa inquired. Was she less sad? Or did she still look out into the golden twilight, close to tears?

Unfortunately, he said, she was more despondent than ever now. Thinking a change might help her, he had sent her with the children the previous autumn to her natal city in the south. After a short time she had in fact improved. She had bought some dresses and had her hair cut in the latest style; her letters had become gay and charming again. He had made the mistake of believing her cured and letting her come back. She had scarcely returned, however, when she slipped into melancholy again. It must be the country itself that was deadly to her with its harshness, its barrenness . . . while with him. . . .

He detached a bit of shale from the rock and sent it skimming over the water.

With him it was quite the opposite. He was not at ease in the South, feeling that the positions were taken there, the stakes laid down and the rivalry cruel under an exterior of false mildness. Only here, it seemed to him, could he see life naked and face to face – hard on the outside, but wasn't that ultimately less inhuman? But it was not their fault, neither hers nor his, that they were as they were. He intended to request transfer to the South.

He turned and saw in Elsa's eyes that pity without comprehension one sometimes sees in the eyes of dogs.

He shook himself and told her that he had crossed the Koksoak for quite another reason. Had she not some slight suspicion what this was?

She gave a calm and confident smile.

"No."

"It's about Jimmy."

Her eyes, like sheltered lakes, black and tranquil in the shadow of a rock, still held no disquiet.

"He hasn't done anything wrong," she said, almost laughing, the broad planes of her cheeks creased with amusement.

He looked at her again, his eyes in their turn so filled with compassion for her that it made her a little anxious finally and she stopped smiling.

"Haven't you thought," he said, "that Jimmy must be sent to school?"

At once Elsa's wide smile returned. That had been looked after, she said. For more than a year now she'd been making a school for him, teaching him as best she could the things she herself had learned – writing, arithmetic, history, the other countries. Would he like to give Jimmy an exam? He knew a lot already.

She was astonished to see that despite this good news the policeman still wore a troubled face. But there was a law, he finally explained, requiring attendance at school from the age Jimmy had now reached.

She would have to go back to live on the other side of the Koksoak and send the boy to the regular school.

When a brief time had slipped by, he looked again at Elsa. The broad face, all amiability and naive friendliness an instant before, was of stone. He was well enough acquainted with the Eskimos to know that nothing could be obtained from them once they had reached this state of inner stiffness. He tried, however, to reason with her.

"Don't you want Jimmy to have a good education so that some day he can take the position that should be his?"

Her eyes turned away, she made no reply, as if she saw no other refuge for herself but obstinate refusal.

The policeman in Roch Beaulieu then informed her, "I can allow you three or four weeks at most for your preparations. After that, if you haven't registered Jimmy at school. . . ."

Then he yielded once more to the kind and compassionate man.

"Elsa, I'll help you find work and a comfortable place to live. What sort of life is it here anyway for a young woman of your age — no distractions, no friends?"

Finally, seeing he would be able to get nothing out of her today, he prepared to leave.

"Don't make it necessary for me to come and get you by force."

She did not accompany him back down to the beach but stood watching him depart from the summit of the rock. And her face, for the first time in her life, was obdurate.

Lying that night on the bench spread with furs, Jimmy heard words that concerned him; though their sense was far from clear, they fascinated him, mixed as they were with a new atmosphere in the hut and the flickering of the embers his mother had hastily blown into life. She paced back and forth, seemingly quite frantic.

"He said he would come and take him by force," she kept saying.

"We'll see about that," said Ian. "When we've three or four days march on them, I'd like to see them catch us. Don't be so upset. We'll have the winter and the tundra on our side. If it will just snow, we're safe."

"But at his age can he stand it?"

"And why not?"

They talked then about the provisions they would need. Elsa began to note them down – tea, sugar, flour, cartridges, matches . . . the list stretched out pleasantly.

On the edge of sleep, Jimmy kept from dozing off by staring at the quivering glow of the fire. He found this atmosphere of flight as delightful as any of the stories Elsa had read to them during the past year. But he remembered that day's visitor with the bright eyes and felt drawn to this man by a natural impulse of confidence.

12

Next day came the heavy snowfall Ian had wanted. He looked jubilant, as if this were a sign of nature's support. He went briskly on with preparations. A great quantity of frozen meat and fish was made into a sort of bundle. The food for the dogs, a string of hard-frozen fish, was tied to the sleigh.

Finally, on a clear, piercingly cold morning, they were ready. The dogs gave tongue on a note that seemed to express exhilaration at leaving everyday existence behind in response to a summons from the unknown.

Of Jimmy, buried in furs at the bottom of the sleigh, nothing could be seen but laughing eyes. From time to time a light low wind lifted the snow, surrounding him in a fine dust, which the sun made dazzling. Jimmy slipped his hand out of the furs and amused himself trying to catch this flying snow. A few paces behind the sleigh Ian ran along on snowshoes, tirelessly keeping up with the dogs.

As soon as they had left the coast, they plunged into a level and limitless white plain. Gone was the land of rock, severe and denuded but still with curves and hollows in which little trees could grow. Here now was the stripped face of creation carried to its ultimate point. From the unending snow not even any wretched grasses emerged. This was the real tundra, Ian explained, with no other covering but its primitive vegetal fleece – the real country of the Eskimos. There was tenderness in his voice, as if he were offering the most hospitable of lands.

If this first day of the journey brought the little boy an intoxication that would impregnate his whole life, this was nothing to his bliss when night came to the tundra.

Yet a short while before, at that hour just after the early disappearance of the sun when bitter cold and a sense of utter desolation spread from all sides, Jimmy had shown some anxiety at finding himself without shelter or warmth. But when he turned a troubled glance towards his uncle Ian, he had been reassured to see the same calm reflective face as always. And in the keen and vigilant eyes, which were examining the surroundings, a decision had seemed to form at that very moment.

They stopped. With his broad-bladed knife, Uncle Ian began to cut large uniform blocks of snow. Elsa helped put them together. Soon Jimmy could watch a small low house taking shape before his eyes. He felt it was being made expressly for him but for the first time in his life his joy did not find its release in shouts and leaps. A crease of gentle astonishment on his forehead, on his lips a smile of delight, he considered it gravely as if, even after seeing it built, he could not quite understand how the igloo came to be there.

They slipped through the low door. Hung from the white dome, the oil-lamp lit up the interior with its subdued flame. Elsa spread the furs to make good warm beds. Soon hot water for tea was singing on the little stove.

Brightened by happiness or perhaps, like the walls of the snow-house, enhanced by the subtle glow of the lamp, the child's eyes were so luminous that Ian exclaimed, laughing, "We could put out the lamp and save oil. The shine in the little fellow's eyes gives all the light we need."

Elsa and Ian laughed for a long time to see Jimmy so enchanted by nothing more really than the ordinary life of the old days. But his delight must have reminded them of their own childhood for, cramped as they were, they stared into space as if lost in dreams and as if around them there were no more walls.

Outside the wind rose. It screamed as it circled the igloo isolated in the endless night. It stopped here and there, like a dog, to sniff out some crack it might enter. Its wailing deepened the little boy's sense of being warm and perfectly safe with people he trusted.

At noon on the third day his impressions and pictures of the journey began to blur, and there was a sharp burning sensation in his throat. At certain moments the silhouette of Uncle Ian, as he ran with regular strides beside the sleigh, seemed as huge and black as the biggest rocks in Fort Chimo. He no longer knew, at other moments, what was laughing in his ears with that terrible resonant and vindictive laugh – the unleashed wind or Uncle Ian himself.

His mother laid her hand on his forehead and said, "He has a fever, Uncle Ian."

His uncle's face became even harder. "In that case we'll race, without a stop if possible, for the coast. Then, if need be, we'll cross over to Baffin Island."

The sick child seized on these words and, as his fever grew, they began to have an enormous charm for him. Soon he was asking again and again whether Baffin Island was in sight and if they would not soon be there.

They stopped and started. Now Jimmy was losing large sections of time and his impressions were disconnected. He would be lying on the racing sleigh, then would open his eyes and find himself, uncomprehending, in another igloo with his mother, her face anxious, begging him to swallow a mouthful of hot tea. He kept struggling to throw off the numerous furs in which she tried to keep him enveloped. At other times he was still struck by the beauty of the flame as it played over the whiteness of the snow-dome and his eyes would follow it waveringly.

One night he woke up to hear his mother and uncle quarrelling.

"We must go back," she was saying. "It's madness to even think of continuing."

"You're like all the others," said Uncle Ian. "Made for captivity."

However, he softened after a moment and promised to search under the snow at daybreak for some of the bark from which his mother used to make an infusion to reduce fever.

"It must certainly be a good remedy," said Elsa mockingly. "The old cemetery would have something to say about that."

She could not seem to find enough bitter things to say about that little cemetery, where she had so loved to walk only a short time before.

Later, she humbled herself in incessant pleading. Ian did not reply.

Even Jimmy tried then to put in his word. Through his delirious mumblings, his mother heard him asking her to listen to Ian and go on to Baffin Island.

To his feverish imagination the distant unknown island had become so mysterious and so beautiful that it was now the target of all his wishes.

Eventually Ian went outside to spare himself further lamentations. He leaned his back against the igloo, his face to some extent protected from the wind. Soon he was as covered with snow as the dogs sleeping all around, their heads protruding from the whitness like so much driftwood. Time passed but he did not move. His body was almost numb. In the opaque night, under lashes heavy with snow, his eyes stared bitterly straight ahead.

At last Elsa came out and, after a long moment's silence, gently touched the black immobile mass under the snow.

"Uncle Ian," she begged. "Come in."

He continued to gaze far into the muffled night. With the tip of her finger she brushed away a little of the snow from the obdurate face.

"It's for you to decide. Come, we will obey you. You're the leader. . . ."

She hesitated imperceptibly.

". . . and the father. . . ."

At last the face, like a half-frozen lump, turned towards her. Ian's wide palm fell upon her, lingered there in a rough imperious caress.

"And the husband?"

She knew then that it was not only anxiety he had been fleeing when he had come out into the bitter cold. Her own senses were stirred by the fierce desire of the man.

They went back in one behind the other. Scarcely half unclothed, they came together in an urgency that flung a huge agitated shadow on the ceiling.

95

Jimmy woke up with a start. He saw that shadow with its inexplicable contortions and gave a scream of fright.

Soon afterwards his mother came to him, her hair undone and her breasts naked, and tried to soothe him in her arms.

It was only a bad dream. There was no animal here, she said.

But the scent of her sickened him. He struggled against her, trying to push her away, and for a long time afterwards he cried desolately.

They had been on the way back to Fort Chimo for quite some time now but Jimmy, who was becoming more and more feverish, was scarcely aware of it. Now they no longer had time to stop to rest and be together in a little house built by Uncle Ian. They must press on relentlessly. The dogs stumbled and howled and, in their exhaustion, attacked one another savagely, adding to their misery.

From time to time the sick child, his chest torn by fits of coughing, opened his eyes. He saw Ian's arm rise and fall, heard the crack of the whip, the groans of the worn-out dogs. Tears sprang to his eyes, which the frost caught at the tips of his lashes and transformed into glittering bubbles.

His mother and Ian were more anxious now, and Uncle Ian struck the lead-dog, Jimmy's favourite Yappy, even more cruelly. The flood of tears increased and, as they froze, almost stopped up his eyes.

Then came a blizzard, without any word this time from Ian. The wind drove him forward as it might have driven some light tuft of vegetation torn from the soil. It pursued everything with the same furious and perpetual movement. Dogs, sleigh, the slanting snow, everything, abused and harried, swept on in a flying blur.

Elsa had managed to thaw the ice that was blinding her child's eyes. He saw this movement of flight – as in a picture his mother had once shown him of Adam and Eve, bowed with shame, fleeing from the Garden of Eden. But to Jimmy the garden to which their backs were now turned and from which they were farther away at every moment, whipped cruelly by the wind, and which they might never manage to find again, was Baffin Island.

They reached the Koksoak at nightfall. Only its edges were frozen, so they were obliged to lighten their load and drive the sleigh at full speed over the new ice, dragging the kayak behind them.

When they reached the open water, they got into the kayak. On this sort of false shoreline they left the dogs which, even half-dead with exhaustion as they were, set up a long griefstricken howl at being left behind.

In turn and sometimes together, they plied the paddles. During the least difficult moments of the crossing Elsa comforted Jimmy, wrapping him more closely in the blankets. They were buffeted by the squalls of snow, drenched by the icy spray. But the wind was with them and they were now assisted by the tide.

At last they reached the frozen rim of the other shore. Here they beached the kayak. First one and then the other carrying Jimmy, they raced over the bumpy surface, urging one another on with brief rough commands as they had earlier urged on the dogs.

The darkness would have been complete without the pale sheen of the snow.

Suddenly, like embers borne on the raging wind, tiny points of light glowed faintly, stretched, disappeared at the whim of the swirling snow, then glimmered briefly again.

These were the first house-lights they had seen for a long time and Elsa greeted them with a leap of the heart.

Soon, although still very weak, the lights shone steadily. They had crossed the Koksoak now and were only steps from those faint gleams that seemed so far away.

At the first Eskimo cabin they obtained a sleigh and some dogs.

They set out again. Now their road was marked out by ever more certain lights. Then a house, all ablaze with its own electricity, loomed up like a constellation with its bright windows and doors.

Elsa ran to the doorstep with Jimmy. A woman in white took him from her arms and went off to put him in a bed.

His mother and Ian now far away from him, he began to cry for help in a weak piteous voice not unlike the complaining of the dogs or the wailing of the air of the night from which they had emerged.

His call was answered by the young nurse. Little by little he learned not to be afraid of her though sometimes still, when he wakened, he wept with grief at not finding the broad dark face of his mother beside him.

One morning, however, he smiled at the girl who looked after him. With the sun playing in her fine hair and grey eyes, he thought her very like himself. He was also becoming used to the bed, which the first day, like some little wild animal, he had feared as a trap.

Next day, when his mother appeared at the door of his room and paused there as if abashed, smiling at him timidly, he examined her at length and with curiosity from head to foot.

It was a bright day and in the flood of light from the window Elsa's pleasant, slightly troubled face was the colour of half-charred wood. As he gazed at her, astonishment spread over Jimmy's face.

He did not greet her as excitedly as on her previous visits. When she approached to rub her nose against his in the Eskimo caress, he even made a tiny movement of withdrawal and looked away impatiently.

Before he left the new Fort Chimo forever, Ian decided to make the little boy a farewell visit.

Seated on a straight chair, uncomfortable and very embarrassed, he looked at the child and no longer knew how to talk to him.

At the end of this visit of almost complete silence, Ian rose and rolled a strand of the golden hair around one of his short, clumsy-looking, yet so skilful fingers.

"So you're cured," he said, "out of danger, as they say," and his expression became aloof and yet grieving. "In any case, you won't have much more need of your old uncle Ian. You'll have teachers far more learned in all matters. . . . Well, good luck, be happy, child of mankind."

The boy raised anxious eyes to the furrowed face on which one more shadow seemed to be marked.

"Uncle Ian," he cried, moved by a confused distress, "you're not going to cross the river today? You'll be back?"

Ian bowed his heavy head in what might have been a sign of assent. He took a few cautious steps towards the door, trying not to slip on the polished floor, and this wariness gave his gait the sort of waddling motion of a bear on its hind legs. Jimmy burst into shrill laughter. Ian started and looked back, scowling, then suddenly his dark face relaxed in an indulgent smile.

Outside the hospital he turned back to have a good look at it once at least before he left. It was only a little wooden house with quarters for the nurse and her assistant on one side and two rooms on the other that could be used, for emergencies or mild illnesses, as sickrooms. But Ian thought he was looking at an imposing building. He considered it with a mixture of irritation and respect, deeply impressed in spite of himself.

He walked on, then stopped a little farther along on the top of a hummock that provided a good view of the greater part of the white men's village. Under the heavy troubled sky, in the snow, winter and wretchedness, it was nothing more than some twenty small houses that had been tossed at random like a handful of dice, some fallen into hollows and others clinging precariously to the crests of the rock that broke through here and there – and over it all fluttered a fine powdering of surface snow.

In Ian's eyes it was a senseless concentration of human life. He could not have spent another night there without risk of smothering. He had been told that he was an old reactionary determined to struggle against what enabled man to advance and perhaps he was, but what could he do about it? His soul was deathly sad that there was no longer any place for him in this world.

He turned towards the Koksoak, his short heavy silhouette in its Eskimo clothes sharp against the lowering sky. He walked very slowly, his face absorbed, the expression in his large prominent eyes mournful. On the shore he halted, looking at the immense frozen expanse before him and he fell into a sort of profound meditation. That the child was cured was good news, of course. What troubled him was the way this cure had been accomplished. A few injections in the frail arm and it was done. Where the people of his country had always failed, despite their patience, despite their prayers, despite their tenderness, the white men succeeded as if playing a game. The fever subsided, the child's breathing eased, he woke up from a quiet sleep, his eyes shining with health. Penicillin – that was what "they" had now, besides everything else, to trap free men.

His dark eyes fixed upon the stretch of ice and snow, Ian thought of the death of his first wife in her twenties, of the second whom he had lost almost as young, of the children he had not managed to save, and all the memories of his life rose in a flood into his throat.

He took a few steps on the pack-ice. For a long time he peered into the distance, shielding his eyes with his hand, searching for some sign of his kayak. The sun suddenly pierced the sullen day and the horizon became dazzling. The wind lifted and puffed the snow, surrounding the immobile figure in fine transparent curtains. With all that sun now, it looked like some graceful or cruel game.

Ian made a movement as if freeing himself from a net. Then, resolutely, he left the shore.

THREE

13

It became time for Elsa to take back her child. Not an instant too soon. He scarcely showed any joy at her visits now, in spite of all the presents she brought him: fruit obtained, one wondered how, as well as little trifles – pebbles from the beach endowed by nature with pleasing shapes or others on which Thaddeus, with a single stroke, had accentuated a resemblance to some living creature.

Jimmy had become very fond of the assistant nurse, a blonde slender girl with grey eyes. Before she showed herself, Elsa would slow her steps anxiously, fearful of hearing them laughing together with that similar laughter that seemed to exclude her.

Then that was all in the past. She took back her son. She also embarked on a new life.

She had, in fact, changed her aim again and was once more firmly on the side of the white men.

It is true that they had helped her in every way possible. Before he left, Roch Beaulieu had given her a sewing-machine and the Catholic mission had used its influence to get her one of the Quonset huts used during the summer by the Government services. The pastor, for his part, provided some furniture and the wife of the director of the Hudson's Bay store a pair of those thick woollen blankets for which the Company was deservedly famous all over the world.

So, a trifle flustered herself by all this, Elsa became from one day to the next the best-housed, most fortunate, most envied Eskimo woman in Fort Chimo.

On the day the hut was to be installed, a difficulty arose, which though seemingly of no great importance would have a decisive effect upon her life to come. Where, in fact, should it be placed? In the Eskimo village? But then Elsa would be "far from everything" and perhaps unpopular with her people in her big hut beside their flimsy shacks. In the white men's village the hut would certainly attract less attention. Elsa did not reflect that if "over there" she would be far from everything, here in the white men's village she would be equally so, in another way.

There was an empty space between the Catholic mission and the Anglican church in the very centre of the village – if you could speak of centre in connection with these houses scattered about here and there at the whim of the hummocks and hollows of the rocky soil.

Elsa's hut possessed a real window. Here she set up her sewing-machine, close to the light, and after a few attempts she was able to operate it and even repair it when she must.

From then on everyone who passed that way along that bit of dusty road – young, old, Father, pastor, whites, Eskimos – would see, whatever the hour, Elsa's bowed face framed in the window as from morning till night without intermission she turned out Eskimo souvenirs.

Adaptable as she was by nature, she now began to live by a new rhythm and from this she never deviated, whole-hearted in this as in all the other ways she'd taken. She rose early, washed Jimmy, combed his hair and sent him off to school, schoolbag on back and dressed in his best suit, the Eskimo outfit having been discarded. She then tidied the hut and ran a wet mop over the floor and even under the beds. Finally, settling down to her work, she began to pedal.

In the course of the next years thousands of small objects came from Elsa's hands and some of them must still exist in various parts of the world. She made them out of woollen cloth or sealskin – the small familiar animals of the tundra or human figures, which she represented often as if poised on the edge of water or sky vaguely dreaming.

The Company bought them from her and disposed of them without difficulty in faraway cities. For the animals she had asked advice from Thaddeus and listened for a long time as he spoke of the attitude of a bear as it considers a scheme, its whole body revealing a sort of cogitation, or the grace of the young seal on the ice-floe when on a sunny day in spring it looks for the first time at the world around.

For the dolls, however, she needed only her own feelings and vivid imagination.

She made them rather on the short side with tightly braided hair, plump cheeks, and cheerful expressions, just as she had been in the days when she used to come home after the movies with Mary Jane, Mildred, and Lily, and the sky before them took on the colour of subdued gold. Not that this memory moved her particularly. It seemed too far away, as far already as the old, old, round mountains on the horizon upon which her eyes found time now and then, between two seams, to rest for a brief moment.

Needless to say she dressed the dolls in the Eskimo style.

"Otherwise what would be their charm?" Mrs. Beard had pointed out to Elsa, who would not now for anything in the world have consented to be seen dressed that way herself.

Later she made parkas by the dozen out of heavy Hudson's Bay point blankets and these, she was told, had an enormous vogue in the country of the GI's. She cut them out of red blankets with broad horizontal black stripes or out of white blankets, some with red stripes and some with green.

A neighbour returned from a trip to Pittsburgh with a tale of seeing someone in a crowd wearing one of Elsa's parkas. She hesitated to believe this, it seemed much too strange. Yet her entire life had been made of the most unlikely events.

A good moment of the day, which habit could never quite dull, came shortly before Jimmy arrived home from school when she put aside her sewing to do a little cooking.

But who would ever have believed that the preparation of meals would require so much effort. She remembered the days of her early childhood when everyone appeased his hunger from the single big dish on the floor. When there was anything to eat in those days, there would be a great deal at a time and the same thing for weeks – raw seal-meat or fish.

Now that Jimmy lived almost entirely among white children and was invited to meals with one or another of them, he wanted, just as they did, to eat nothing but hamburger.

She had tried to serve him other sorts of meat but he pushed the plate disdainfully away. And beef, reared and nourished in pastures as distant as the moon and flown in by plane, was an exorbitant price. There was some, however, at the hotel – a sort of barracks in the sand—for those dignitaries whose descent from planes, one hand batting at the clouds of mosquitoes, the other trying to keep their hats from flying away in the wind, Winnie had found so entertaining.

She used to go and buy a few pounds from the hotelkeeper, who of course took a cut. Part of it she would then leave in the hotel refrigerator. For another annoying thing about hamburger is that it spoils very quickly. And cold to preserve foodstuffs, once summer has come, is precisely what is lacking in the sub-Arctic. So Elsa had either to go and get meat as she needed it from the hotelkeeper, who wasn't too gracious about this, or carry it all away at once and then, a day or two later when it had begun to thaw out, put it in the refrigerator of the Fathers, who had generously offered her its use. She got her meat in one place, kept it in another, and expended almost more effort and inventiveness to serve Jimmy hamburger patties than a whole family on the tundra in the old days had required to obtain food for a month. As well, she often felt ashamed when she went to get her meat at the Fathers' and found them at table eating frugally and she hoped that she too would own a refrigerator some day. But first she would need a home electricity plant and that was certainly not for tomorrow.

She made good money, but on the road she had taken each small improvement called for ten others. In addition, Jimmy was always asking for nickels and dimes to buy coke, chewing gum, or comics. What the Hudson's Bay gave her with one hand it seemed to take from her with the other.

"But it's always like that and it's far worse in the South," Mrs. Beard told her. "You have no idea what a crazy life they live there."

Yet Madame Beaulieu had said it was the most delightful life imaginable.

"Don't you believe any such thing," said tall Mrs. Beard very firmly. "I wouldn't live there again for anything in the world."

She often congratulated Elsa for being able to speak a little English, which she claimed was the language of the country. On the other hand, Madame L'Ecuyer, the wife of the new policeman and as vehement as Madame Beaulieu had been melancholy, maintained that the language of the country was French. And all the while Father Eugene was ruining his eyesight making an alphabet for the Eskimo language as spoken at Fort Chimo, maintaining that this was the first language of the country.

Elsa had scarcely time to make sense out of this wrangle and meanwhile simply did her best to be understood by everyone.

Another good moment in the day came in the evening when Jimmy dawdled over a sandwich of the good white bread, ready sliced and delivered like everything else by plane. Elsa had been careful not to acquire a taste for it herself lest she find it too hard to do without it later, for, as Thaddeus pointed out, who would continue to eat the bread of the past once he has tasted that of today?

Rather late, her long day behind her at last, she would go to the doorstep and shout towards the children playing in a close, solitary little group against the darkening sky.

"Hi, Jimmy! It's time."

Sometimes he needed coaxing and at other times came running.

She would close the door for the night upon a home of their own such as they had never had before. It was even pleasanter and more intimate than Uncle Ian's and very much brighter. The oil lamp cast a patch of light full upon the table, which was covered with oilcloth that Elsa scrubbed with scouring powder. In fact it was so clean and shining in her hut that few of the other Eskimos could bear to stay more than five minutes. They would stop on their way to or from the store just long enough to look around curiously. Soon Elsa would see a sort of tiredness on their faces and with it the desire to be elsewhere.

Only Thaddeus forced himself, out of sheer goodness of heart, to remain for quite a long time, though he was silent through almost his entire visit. When he arrived – and likewise when he left – a peculiar reflex made him wipe his feet on the straw mat at the door, even in the driest weather. This little movement, which Elsa finally noticed one day, succeeded better than anything in opening her eyes to the distance that was being established between herself and her own people, though without her volition.

For several days after that she felt worn-out by the weight of too many possessions and even less fond of the big hut. If she tried to look into the still cloudy future, she felt that it was bound to separate her more and more from her real nature and sweep her finally far from herself. She could form no clear picture of where she was going. If, on the other hand, she looked back in the direction from which she had come, she realized that it was impossible for her to return to that way of living. She was condemned, she saw, to move farther and farther into the unknown.

However, almost every evening by a sort of magic when she had Jimmy all to herself, she got back her sense that she was indeed on the right road. Jimmy would open his books and start his homework. When he asked her to help him with his spelling and she found she still could, happiness would glow on her broad, moved face.

Then it would be time to sleep.

No matter how insolent or capricious he had been during the day, he always calmed down when his mother put him to bed and took up the thread of the long story she was telling him night after night.

She herself would become simple and confident as she repeated the old stories of the time of her own childhood.

When at last he was asleep, his face smooth and pure, a lock of hair fallen over his forehead, she would gaze down at him, no longer remembering the anger he turned upon her whenever she opposed his whims and demands.

14

When he was eleven she bought him a bicycle, to put
him on an equal footing with his playmates – Bob and
Jules, the sons of the representative of Indian Affairs,
and John and Alistair, those of the director of the
Hudson's Bay.

The bicycles were small in size, half brilliant red
and half glittering chrome, with long strips of multicoloured plastic flapping from the handlebars. They
also had screeching horns which the children sounded
continually even when there was nothing in their way
but a poor stupefied dog.

They would race abreast or single file along the
old Army road, now almost all crumbled away but still
the only surface by far that lent itself to any extent
to the bicycle.

Pedalling with all their might, their hair almost
carried away by the wind, they would come to the end
of the road, after which were pebbles to pierce their
tires, and then turn and pedal back in the opposite
direction. At this precise point there stood, so to speak
permanently, watching the arrival and departure of
the parade, a little group of Eskimo children, their
eyes wide with amazement, accompanied by their
equally spellbound dogs. All of them that summer –
the white children when they arrived in sight of the
little Eskimos and the latter when they saw the band

of "town" children return – seemingly never wearied of the diverting spectacle they provided for one another.

At the shrill uproar that announced the return of the cyclists Elsa would look up briefly. She would begin to watch the bit of road that was visible from her sewing-machine. At a particular moment Jimmy would appear in her narrow field of vision. If it occurred to him to glance to that side, he could see the smiling but always slightly anxious face of his mother. When he was in a good humour he would raise his hand in greeting as he passed, shouting over the rasp of the sand under his wheels, "Hi!"

She would smile, completely satisfied with him. No more than this was needed to send warm delighted blood into the high prominent cheekbones of her face, which was beginning to lose some of its freshness. She would go back to her dolls with less weariness. All was well. Today Jimmy was in Alistair's gang; he would improve his English and learn a thousand other useful things. Tomorrow he would be on the side of the French-speaking children and that would be equally good and profitable.

In all that summer she did not find an instant to go and listen to the Koksoak. Day after day she told herself she must go, that it was senseless to let a whole summer slip away without filling her ears at least once with its consoling murmur. But she now had an electrical generator and this progress in a sense enslaved her. A sixty watt bulb over her sewing-machine gave so much light that she could now go on sewing far into the evening. Her dolls were still in demand. And, as Mrs. Beard said, she mustn't disappoint the "customers." Moreover, Jimmy had cast his eyes upon a cowboy outfit displayed in the same window where not long ago she herself had caught sight one day of the little snowsuit through which everything perhaps had begun. So she shouldn't blame her child too much. He was only following in her footsteps; she understood him as well as she did herself.

Nevertheless, she had to admit that these months were among the happiest of her life, for she had not for a single moment needed to worry about Jimmy, since she always knew where he was – either in the saddle racing down the old road of the GI's or dead tired, sleeping with clenched fists under her care.

In the autumn Winnie died – in the old way, you might say, in any case not in her bed as she had always predicted she would, although properly speaking she did not have a bed but only a pallet on the floor. She was found in the sand, leaning against a rusty oil drum, a cigarette dangling from her lips, her eyes turned towards the Koksoak, which so much of her life had been spent in watching, and she wore in death almost the same expression that had been hers in recent years – a little disappointed, a little lost, her right eye almost closed because of the smoke of her cigarette. Only the smoke was missing.

Yet at the funeral the Reverend Hugh Paterson found many true and moving things to say about this poor, quite ordinary life. He may have been recalling his own childhood in the Yorkshire dales – the cottage with its floor of beaten earth, the gorse-covered hills, the unfettered wind – for he spoke of Winnie's existence as if he knew it through his own flesh and his own human sorrow.

To the handful of Eskimos listening to him in bewilderment, startled to hear so much good spoken now of this poor old woman, he said that all life is a struggle to go beyond one's limits, attain something better, make one's self over, and that Winnie had not failed in her own way to conform to this law and this duty.

For the white men it was difficult enough, he said, to distinguish, in the ever-moving race of events, between what carried men forward and what did not. For the Eskimos it was a thousand times more arduous and delicate. Winnie had been caught, as few human beings are, between the cruel blades of the times: what to change, what to keep? She had struggled as best she could, had often been mistaken but had done her utmost to improve herself, and this would be counted for her.

Archibald, astounded, looked as if he were wondering whom the pastor was discussing with so much respect. Thaddeus, who was now almost blind, his face calm and beautiful, was smiling as if at obvious truths.

For Elsa this had been the occasion to christen the new flowered dress she had copied from a picture in a mail-order catalogue. She was wearing high-heeled shoes and, perched somewhat insecurely on her heavy hair, one of the odd little hats Madame Beaulieu had given her before she left, saying, "Elsa dear, could you just tell me what I could have been thinking when I brought all these hats up here?" Beside her was Jimmy in his first long trousers, shifting about and muttering that he found the sermon interminable. Patient though she always was with him, she told him he must behave himself. She was beginning to be concerned that at church or among his relatives he so often looked bored or scornful.

She felt sad. The death of her mother affected her more deeply than she would have expected. After all, she had not cared all that much about Winnie when she was alive. Perhaps the fine words that were being spoken about her were drawing her at last from the general indifference in which she had lived so long that no one saw her any more.

Now Elsa "saw" her mother. She saw her from behind, walking along the beach, a little thread of cigarette smoke preceding her or following her, according to the direction of the wind, for this had long been her only companion.

She had tried one day to stop Jimmy on the old Army road, to give him a tender word or perhaps an old, half-melted candy. He had brushed her aside with impatient hoots of his horn and raced by with such speed that the wind of his passage made her stagger, since she was already very weak.

Elsa continued to see her, always in the same place and yet always on the move, alone and puny in the bare and silent immensity of the Eskimo country. Then all at once her gaze sharpened and she leaned forward as if for better sight of some intuitive and troubling image. Did it come to her from the future and was it herself she saw, taking Winnie's place in the interminable and always solitary procession of the generations? Surrounded by her own people who loved her and with her son at her side, she still seemed to everyone forlorn and dejected.

Just then the Reverend Hugh Paterson terminated his eulogy with the words that Winnie was now in everlasting peace.

Had these words become in themselves incomprehensible to Elsa? Or much too strange when applied to Winnie, who had spent her life on the roads – or on what passed for roads here. Elsa gave the pastor a baffled look in which he thought he read that she did not know, did not understand how one ought to live though she had tried every day.

But who does know, his eyes seemed to answer her, who does know how to live?

15

The following summer Jimmy's mother gave him the glove, mask, ball, and bat of a baseball-player. The children had forsaken their bicycles almost entirely in their passion for this game, which Alistair had taught them on his return from a stay in the city. They played this too in the middle of the old Army road from which they had to scatter only at long intervals when the Father's jeep or the Nordair station wagon went by.

From her window Elsa could not see the children, who were hidden by an outcropping of rock, but when they were excited or counting up the score she heard them. So when Jimmy came home in the late afternoon, she knew who had won and who lost and could make a show of understanding the game a little for the joy of hearing him tell her about it and sometimes, rather loftily, explain the rules.

During that summer also she might have been able – to use an expression of the pastor's, who was urging this – to "make herself a new life," though to her life didn't seem the sort of thing one made. Wasn't it rather like the river, with no choice, once its course was set, of not flowing henceforth, as the land sloped, to the sea?

However, on an evening of gilded sky like those of her youth, she put on the dress she had worn the day of her mother's funeral and her high-heeled shoes and, still very short beside Jimmy, went down to the hall at the Catholic mission. From the doorway she began to smile timidly at all those present. Among these was a young Eskimo widower named William, on a visit from his home on the coast, who found her much to his liking and kept glancing at her with sparkling eyes. Elsa did not take this amiss and, when her eyes chanced to meet his, she looked quickly away with a smile as excited as a young girl's, which lit up her face and made her look very much younger.

When the film, *Ben Hur*, was over, she was joined at the exit by the young man, who proceeded to walk beside her in silence. Their heads bowed, they smiled questioningly at one another. Elsa's flesh quivered with a new sensation. A sensation in no way resembling the anguish Ian's tragic passion had roused in her or her union, in surprise and confusion, with the GI. The emotion that came over her now might have suggested the silent and gentle unfolding of a new leaf or of a flower in the sand. She continued to smile, keeping her face turned slightly away and swinging her arms.

Then along came Jimmy, slipping between his mother and the young Eskimo with an insolent look for the latter. He may have intuitively sensed a threat to the tyrannical power he had held over her since his birth. Or was it just one of the brief sudden bursts of tenderness he showed for her upon occasion? At any rate, he seized her hand and made a great fuss over her, talking about the film, suddenly with a thousand things to say. She did her best to divide her attention between the speechless William and the talkative and possessive child until suddenly she perceived that the young man had fallen behind and was now gazing after them with an expression of regret.

For several days she too seemed to feel regret and was absent and dreamy. But this was all she would ever know that in any way approached love. A little later she learned that William was married again, to a girl from a village on James Bay.

After freeze-up she bought Jimmy a complete set of hockey equipment, but by now there were not enough white children in the village to make up a team. John and Alistair had been sent to the city to continue their studies. The next year it was the turn of the policeman's children. Jimmy was alone.

The Eskimo children would probably not have borne him any malice for spurning them before, but he did not want to have anything to do with them and always walked away as soon as school was over with a none too friendly nod.

He was still growing very quickly. He was soon all arms and legs – long, slight, and skinny, with brittle-looking wrists and a thin stalk of a neck. Never before had Elsa seen a human creature stretch like this, all height without breadth, and she was sometimes fearful it would never stop. She herself had begun to thicken and sometimes already, when she did not watch herself, she would slip for a moment into Winnie's gait, heavy-footed and stooped.

As he grew so endlessly and too quickly, Jimmy also became morose and taciturn. He would crouch at the back of the hut, reading or pretending to read for hours. Or on Saturdays he would go and roam about all day without giving her the slightest explanation.

Once she dared to ask him where he was off to like this without even taking anything to eat, but he flung her a hostile look and departed without a word. He was now a full head taller than she was and his blue eyes, in which she had once often seen the clarity of the sky, now reminded her of ice.

One day, however, she decided to follow him, keeping well behind him and hiding, whenever his steps slowed, in one of the occasional tufts of vegetation. They arrived thus, a fair distance from one another, not far from the beach and the Eskimo village. She then lost sight of him and had walked quite openly for a moment when he rose suddenly from a clump of bushes, accusing her of always spying on him. Couldn't she just leave him alone for once? The great distress she had time to read in his eyes almost overwhelmed her and she went back to the hut, her face anguished, as if she were the author of this inexplicable sorrow.

Soon afterwards she learned that the boy had been going to see Thaddeus and this gave her hope for her child.

For no one had such a gift as this blind old man for showing others what their own eyes could not see.

Jimmy did in fact still go quite often to watch Thaddeus at work. He would enter, sit down and sometimes let a good moment slip by without speaking or betraying his presence by the slightest sound, perhaps thinking he might some day trick the keen attention of the blind man. But all of a sudden he would hear himself asked in a quite natural voice and without any hesitation, "What do you think of my birds today, little one?"

Or, "Give me some advice about the beak of this young vulture. Is it sufficiently curved?"

Sometimes, thinking that he could indeed guide the old man, Jimmy would consent to give his advice.

"The beak is a bit too heavy."

With delicate slow movements Thaddeus would touch the legs, the beak, the neck.

"You may be right. And the wings?"

"The wings are perfect."

A smile never failed to light up the old man's face when anyone spoke well of his work.

But sometimes Jimmy would be sulky and refuse to unseal his lips. He would watch the knotted hands rise as if to model – or capture? – living forms. Sometimes they would fall back in discouragement.

"Today I can't 'see'."

Neighbours looked after Thaddeus, brought him food, cleaned his hut to some extent and never left him without attention. But help him to see? When there was no wind nor rustle of grass, not even any of those tenuous sounds that revealed to his acute ear the life of nature, then Thaddeus said he was in the dark and would sit on his stoop, waiting patiently and feeling a little lonely.

One day when Jimmy arrived without a sound and found the old man sitting with inert hands, he was about to withdraw without speaking when Thaddeus said suddenly, "Little one! Won't you stay for a while?"

"Little one!" Jimmy repeated with some derision.

"Oh I know you're very tall," said Thaddeus. "Taller already than any Eskimo of the old days or even today. You're the tallest of us all."

Jimmy listened with a sombre face. Suddenly he made up his mind.

"Thaddeus, when I was small you said you couldn't do my likeness because it escaped you. Now I'm taller than any of you. Thaddeus, where did I come from? Why am I here?"

"Where you come from, my child, I'm not too sure – nor of where you are going. On the other hand, I believe I know why God put you among us."

"And why would he have put me here?"

"For our joy," Thaddeus answered tenderly. "And also for our perpetual astonishment."

Shortly afterwards Jimmy's teacher sent word for Elsa to come and see her.

Elsa went into a splendid spacious building, as far from the school of her childhood as she was herself from the child she had been at that time, dressed in Eskimo clothes and smiling continually. She went along a corridor, glancing into classrooms that looked as bright behind their walls of glass as shelters for the nurture of delicate plants. But she felt too fearful and anxious to admire them as she might have liked. And with reason. Jimmy's teacher was very displeased with him. He was becoming a problem and quite truthfully she no longer knew how to handle him.

Elsa made a show of understanding, said she would do her best to find a way and managed to keep control of herself until she had escaped this woman who, while accusing Jimmy, had looked as if she held his mother responsible.

Then it was as if everything were collapsing – the patient edifice of her life, the mountain of Eskimo dolls she had worked on by day and by night. And what was there left that was of any use to her?

On her way home she chanced to meet Jimmy, who looked, at first sight of her, as if he wanted to slip away but finally let her approach. She tried to be severe.

"Why do you run away from school? Such a lovely school! So gay, so bright! That has cost the great government that governs us so much money!"

He looked at her with a sort of pity and then interrupted her. It was just a school for Eskimos. He'd had enough of being with those broad faces. Since his friends had left, school was no longer school.

In her shame and stupefaction she could find nothing to reply. As she served him his meal that evening she returned gently to the attack. Why not associate with the Eskimos? They loved him. They accepted him as one of their own. And if the whites were scornful, well, too bad!

But all at once she sensed the uselessness of going on. Several times already she had felt that she was being stared at by her own child with the same cool measuring quality she had seen in the eyes of the soldiers as they filed by on the icy road. Today there was scarcely any more doubt: Jimmy was looking at her as a stranger.

A little later he went so far as to ask her who his real mother was: had there not been some mix-up with the babies at the hospital after his birth?

She understood then that in his shame at having her for mother he had made up stories as she used to do when she was young, on her way home after the movies.

At last one day she believed it best to inform him of the truth. To give herself a little strength, she sat down at the sewing-machine. She folded her hands and, letting her eyes wander about the room, began her account: the lovely tender Arctic evening, the sky all gold, the little group returning from the cinema. In spite of herself, her eyes smiled faintly, for these memories had grown gentle with the years. Or was it for herself, so young and naive at that time, that she felt affection? She came to her meeting with the young soldier of the beating heart. She caught Jimmy's voracious, anxious look and, almost without noticing, she began to invent – what the young man had said, her own reply, how they had laughed together and walked hand in hand, he a handsome appealing boy who told her about his life in Mississippi . . . and she, well, she had listened. They had not been able to marry, since the Army did not permit marriage between the GI's and the Eskimo girls. So they had so to speak married one another by their own choice one evening. . . .

"Where?" asked Jimmy abruptly and she lost the thread of the story, which she was perhaps beginning to believe a little, for suddenly her eyes dulled, she saw the rib of naked rock that cut off her view some distance from her window, and her shoulders slumped.

Then Jimmy asked her for the name of the soldier from Mississippi.

She tried to draw herself from the disturbing reveries into which she had plunged as a bird might plunge into thick fog. She no longer knew, she said. It was a difficult name to remember.

When she finally emerged from her journey into the past and looked about her, she saw Jimmy racing on his bicycle along the old broken Army road, as if it might take him somewhere.

Here and there some wretched grasses had managed to pierce the asphalt and now formed small islets of sickly green.

A little later she glanced at the round-faced doll at which she had mechanically resumed work and suddenly she had no more heart for such a task.

Aimlessly, not yet knowing where she would go, she put on one of her hats and set out, not by way of the village but by the shortcuts through the rubble of rock, across the silent country towards the Koksoak.

When she reached it, she looked searchingly to both sides of the immense beach but could see no sign anywhere of a human being. She sat down then and, her eyes on the flowing water, tried to think. She was aware only of a patient perplexity, a sort of timid questioning that rose from the depths of her soul seeking to know whether there was someone at the end of the world waiting to welcome weary travellers. This seemed in no way connected with religious instruction or the answers given for everyone; it was as if the sole important question had been asked of Elsa personally and must be answered by her. But she was at present so tired, so far behind in sleep, that even sorrow and anxiety could not keep her from dozing off in brief snatches of release. So mercifully she sank into an instant of oblivion, sitting in the ocean wind, wearing the frivolous hat that Madame Beaulieu had bought, as she had bought so many others, to help restore her taste for life.

When she wakened, the hat had been carried away by the wind; she searched for it, having room in her grief for regret that she had probably lost such a valuable hat. Unable to find it, she went back with dragging steps to the hut. For where else was there to go? No doubt Jimmy too would learn this soon. Sorrow, rebellion, bitterness – it all ends by going back home.

Indeed he was there already, spurred on by hunger, for as she came in she saw him force down a mouthful of something that stuck in his throat and he was perhaps hiding a bit of bread behind his back. His eyelids were swollen and his face streaked with a mixture of dried tears and dust. Simply out of habit, she handed him a damp cloth to wash himself. Then she opened her little cupboard and took out what she needed to fix him a meal.

Neither of them spoke. When the food was ready, he sat in his place at the table and let her serve him.

She moved back and forth, glancing at him furtively. His look of misery so overwhelmed her that, as she passed him, she forgot herself to the extent of putting out her hand to brush a lock of hair from his forehead, as she used to do when he was little. He stopped her with a cutting glance.

She slept that night at the far end of the hut on a bearskin spread upon the floor. Because she was cold perhaps or felt too much alone, she drew her knees up to her chin in the timorous posture of the human being before birth.

She heard Jimmy crying during the night. She ached to go to comfort him and tell him that all sorrow passes but she did not dare and felt that she might never dare to do so again.

16

Jimmy had always been fascinated by planes and was in the habit of running onto the airstrip at the arrival or departure of the North Star that touched down at Fort Chimo three times a week. A natural bent for mechanics and his hours spent watching the ground crew had made him already quite skilful when he was asked one day to lend a hand in an emergency. Jimmy consented eagerly and made an excellent impression. He was congratulated, which seemed to delight him. From then on his most serene hours were those he spent in the maintenance hangar, always ready to help out and add to his knowledge when he could. It seemed as if he would follow the example of Archibald and his uncle Lawrence, who were both first-class mechanics.

At home he continued to keep his mother at a distance. He came in only to wash, put on the clean clothes she provided for him, and sleep. Side by side in that narrow hut, they still contrived to live as strangers, no longer knowing anything, you might say, of one another's thoughts and feelings.

Now and again a small sign made Elsa think that everything was going to change and that all feeling of affection for her could not be dead in Jimmy's heart. She watched her child's face continually as one sometimes watches the sky for the first hint of a clearing.

One evening he did not come home at the hour when all activity ceased at the landing field. Soon everyone had gone home for the night and there were no more comings or goings on the vast open land. Anxious now, Elsa went on waiting, crouched in the hut, holding her breath for moments at a time the better to catch the faintest sound of a step that would tell her of Jimmy's return.

She rose finally and went to the doorstep to scrutinize the cheerless landscape. It was bathed in the sort of twilight that lasts in the North until dawn in its turn spreads over the sky, one might say, almost the same mat clarity of transparent night. In this light shapes can be discerned from far away but, though Elsa looked in all directions, she saw no movement anywhere. The starless sky, the lifeless earth, the dim horizon – all seemed to her that night to be stricken by an appalling immobility. She could not even see the furtive outline of a husky, though it was rare that two or three did not run loose at night, despite the order that had been given to the Eskimos to keep their dogs tied up.

Peering into this desert, for that was what her own land now seemed to her, Elsa could not stop asking herself the agonizing question: Where could Jimmy have found refuge and with whom, since he had wilfully estranged himself from the Eskimos, who were perhaps his only friends? For had the white men, she now asked herself, ever really considered him one of their own?

In the morning she decided to go and prowl around the buildings at the airstrip. Her disquiet grew when she did not find Jimmy among the men at work. However, instead of steeling herself to step forward and question them about her child, the instant she saw them look at her inquiringly she hurried away, bowing her head with a guilty expression.

She went down to the beach and began to walk from cove to cove, assuring herself that this was the place to look, for she had just remembered that from his earliest childhood Jimmy had been inclined, like herself, to seek refuge when troubled beside the Koksoak. All that day, as she wandered endlessly along the river, she asked herself countless times whether it was from the Eskimo side of his nature that her child had inherited his love for water, clouds, and daydreams. She might have given him only this, and it would still have been a great help to him in his passage through life.

Each cabin she came to she entered. She confined herself to a searching and griefstricken glance and departed without explanation. What would have been the need? They all understood and gazed after her for a moment with a look of compassion or of slight mockery perhaps, though without real malice.

She spent another night on the sill of her cabin, like a shadow, without stirring, straining after the smallest sound.

A few stars eventually appeared in the depths of the pale sky, themselves as pale as the reflections of stars.

Huddled on the doorstep, her head between her hands, Elsa was no longer aware of anything in the outside world. As if her brain had no other function now but to project images of the time of her happiness, it showed her Jimmy again and again when he was still young and winning, still loved her and displayed his love. She watched these images of tenderness pass through her mind and could not believe they were only shadows of what was lost. At times, recall-

ing a saying of Winnie's: "When we see things clearly
in our heads, it is because we no longer hold them in
our hands," she tried to push the memories away, as
enemies, but it was useless. The tender images flowed
into her as the water of the ocean flows into the river
at high tide.

Next morning she made up her mind to go to the
maintenance hangar at the airstrip and question the
foreman.

He too, he said, had been wondering what had
happened to Jimmy since they had not seen him for
two days. He advised Elsa to inform the policeman of
the disappearance.

As she walked, preparing what she would say, ges-
ticulating a little to help herself think, trying out a
sentence aloud from time to time, it still had not occurred to her that she was about to inform against
Jimmy. She realized this suddenly when she stood below the Beaulieus' old house, so full of memories for
her. Roch Beaulieu's successor was also held to be
affable and kind, but he might not be fully acquainted
with Elsa's past. He would be most astonished that she
had a slim blue-eyed boy as a son. Her instinct cau-
tioned her to be very careful what she said since the
future of her unhappy child depended upon it, and she
was very afraid she might not be equal to so complex
and difficult a task. She paced back and forth in front
of the house on the knoll, unable to make up her mind
to continue, without thinking that her behaviour
would give her away to eyes that were almost certainly watching her movements from above.

In fact Maurice L'Ecuyer, seated at his picture
window reading the city newspapers, had seen the approach across the long rocky expanse of the familiar
little silhouette – for who now did not know Elsa with

her high-heeled shoes, her odd hats, and queer appearance? – and was beginning to be troubled by the sight of her constantly on the point of climbing the stairs and constantly changing her mind.

In the end he went out to fetch her. He had just been advised of Jimmy's disappearance, he told her. Moreover, someone remembered seeing him the evening before last in the vicinity of the departing aircraft. So it was not difficult to imagine that he had managed to hide himself among the bundles that were being loaded on board. It was simply a matter now of alerting Roberval and it would probably not be long before the fugitive was apprehended.

"Roberval," she said, turning the word over with mistrust.

Her face, at the mention of hiding among the bundles, had not been able to hold back an expression very close to admiration. Now it showed only cruel embarrassment. Would it not be better, she suggested, for her to go to Roberval first and see if Jimmy wanted to come back?

"If he wants to come back? But how old is Jimmy? Fifteen?"

She lowered her eyes in assent.

"In that case there's no need to ask his opinion. You're still for the time being the head of the family."

She looked so helpless that the policeman, thinking like so many others before him that he could assist her, said charitably, "It's none of my business, Elsa, but couldn't you handle the boy a little better? Have you ever as much as refused him anything?"

She gave him an almost vindictive glance, looking for a brief moment as if she were about to fight back for once. But this interval of bitterness soon passed and with pensive little nods, her eyes gazing into the distance, she seemed to accept the rebuke.

That very evening the policeman sent her word that Jimmy had been found. At Roberval he had attracted attention very quickly by his appearance, his sudden passion for pinball machines, and his efforts to attach himself to a group of young people whom he had trailed through the streets.

From these curious details Elsa tried to form some idea of this unknown place where her son had gone and of what its charm might have been for him. Was there just some way she could obtain for him here what he had liked in Roberval? Pinball machines – she would first have to discover what those were.

She went to wait for him hours ahead of time, clean and neatly dressed, practising a smile that would make it immediately clear to Jimmy that nothing mattered but the joy of seeing him again, but the high wind dishevelled her and gradually the smile wore off.

Jimmy appeared on the ramp. He seemed to have aged by ten years. Forehead creased, lips tight, he reminded Elsa of the GI's on days when they had been punished. He would never believe that she had been more on his side than not in his flight and had in any case done nothing to bring him back by force.

She knew then that he was lost to her, that it was only a question of time now before he managed to escape forever. For very little she would have schemed with him, confident that in this at least she could be useful to him, with all the tricks atavism had taught her for putting pursuers off the track.

From the occasional scraps of confidence Jimmy let slip she discovered that it had been his idea to reach the USA, which he thought of as a sort of paradise. The only moments when his young, almost always hostile face brightened somewhat was when he talked about that country. To give him pleasure, Elsa took to speaking well of it at every turn, implying that she would be capable herself of setting out one day to try to reach those United States with him. Without going as far as complete trust, for she had betrayed him once, Jimmy from time to time revealed a few more of his wild hopes. Overjoyed that he was willing to talk to her even a little, Elsa was ready to approve even the most senseless schemes. This time of semi-complicity between them might have been the best they had had if it had been made to endure.

The following year he was much better able to handle things and must have gone straight to some large city, Montreal perhaps, where search was more difficult. The Fort Chimo police informed Elsa that they were turning Jimmy's dossier over to their superiors since the case no longer concerned them.

Months passed and no trace of the boy was ever found. At times this was a source of pride to Elsa. How he had made them run, the policemen and all the others – served them right! She imagined him as having finally reached the country of the GI's and found his equals – men who were all tall, strong and happy, and without fear. It seemed to her that she had only one chance of ever seeing Jimmy again: if he attained his goal. In that case, he would want her to know. Whatever anyone said, she knew her child well; when he made a discovery, he had always returned to show it to her. She could still hear him sometimes in her memory, calling in a shrill voice, "See what I've got!" He would run to her, open his hand and display a small stone that had been delicately modelled by weather, tide, and storm.

17

Little by little Elsa's now aimless life began to come apart as what had been its mainspring and provided its meaning unwound. She slipped by stages into the idleness and tendency to endless daydreaming that were probably the basis of her character and had been surmounted only by a perpetual impetus of love.

She gave up sewing almost completely and when after several months she found herself short of money, in order to continue to feed herself, more or less, she sold her sewing-machine. Only when Mary Jane came to carry it away in a sort of wheelbarrow did Elsa appear to rouse for an instant from her indifference. She fixed upon the old machine a gaze in which life and memories seemed to struggle against breaking mists. Not for long. Her face became once more dull and apathetic. After her sewing-machine she let her fine woollen blankets and her curtains go for very little.

The hut was almost as empty as on the day Elsa had moved in and begun to work unrestingly to make it a home. So, she seemed to be thinking as she let her eyes wander over the stripped walls, life is spent in creating a home that in an instant is unmade. As if she now found something amusing in the spectacle of her own life, or of all life, she fell into the habit of laughing silently, thumping herself on the thighs, as Winnie used to do only a short time before.

She finally abandoned the hut and went back to live in the Eskimo village. On the beach, at some distance from all the others, she found a shack that had stood empty for years and was thus available to anyone who wanted it. Elsa made some sketchy repairs to the poorly closing door and the leaking roof. When her nearest neighbours came to inquire whether she needed anything, she told them she had more than was necessary; the less one owned the better. Her princely hut and the luxury in which she had lived now seemed to her shackles; she could no longer understand how she had endured them. And besides, for whom would she take so much trouble? Thaddeus was dead, Winnie was dead, Ian had vanished without anyone ever knowing whether he had finally reached Baffin Island. Archibald and Lawrence worked at Frobisher Bay and seldom sent news. A human family can come apart more quickly than certain pairs of birds that spend their whole lives together. Now she had nothing of her own but the river and she listened to it unceasingly, sitting on the stones or lying on the floor of her shack, her face turned towards the out of doors.

She slept fully clothed. She no longer had beds to make or even any meals to prepare, for she ate whatever she chanced to have, a mouthful at random when she felt very hungry. There was only one household task to which she remained faithful, her laundry; she washed on the beach in a tub of water heated over a fire of rubbish. Sometimes she had old tires to burn. Through their evil black smoke she would be seen only dimly, stirring her fire.

She continued also for some time to wash and change on Sunday and then, presentable in one of her clean dresses, she would walk to church, avoiding groups and keeping for as long as possible close to the river. She would take a seat in the back pew and scarcely ever raised her eyes any more to the pastor during the sermon. She was always the last to leave and would let all the others outstrip her, as if not to have to respond any longer to human solicitude or curiosity.

Only when she was down to her last bit of food would she resign herself to seeking work among the white men, and she would rarely commit herself for more than two or three days at one time. She who did hardly any scrubbing at home would then begin to chase dirt with a vigour still slightly reminiscent of the good little worker of old. One day when she was housecleaning at the Catholic mission, Father Eugene, after first reproaching her, as everyone did, for "letting herself go," suggested that she stay. She would have a fixed salary, assured employment, and security.

She heard him out, her face strained and her forehead puckered, as if he were speaking in a foreign language. A salary, assured employment, security — what would she do with all that? When she wanted only to buy with the price of her labour the right to do nothing for a while beside the river and feel, like the river, borne along and free. . . .

But after these days of effort it was sometimes difficult for her to sink back into her lazy fluid dreaminess. Memories badgered her, the habits of cleanliness and hygiene she had once learned struggled to be reborn, her movements became fidgety once more. She would have to walk for days, her head forward and her shoulders stooped, taking herself to task, before she could wear away her renewed grief and the desire to take her life in hand again and try, with more pain to herself, to direct it towards some changing, impossible, forever incomprehensible goal.

The years, however, were in the long run benevolent and at last allayed these faint stirrings as well as her regrets.

Of her possessions from the time of her splendour she now had only her little radio and to this she was still attached, perhaps because it was connected with the world from which the GI had come and to which the child had gone. From time to time she forgot it, lost somewhere under a pile of skins and rags. Then it would occur to her to dig it out and listen to what it might once more have to recount to her of the always surprising acts and movements of the people elsewhere.

And so it was that the news found its way to her one evening that several divisions of GI's had just disembarked in a country called Vietnam.

At mention of GI's she sat up. Her face brightened. She stared voraciously at the radio as if, by sheer persistence, she could make it give some fuller explanation. But it had already passed on to other things.

No matter: that name of an unknown country, tossed so suddenly into the hut, was not going to leave her in peace often or for long.

She ran at once to the nearest of her neighbours who possessed a radio. Had they also heard the extraordinary news? No, they replied, nothing in the least extraordinary – just the same old fuss as always that the white men called the cold war.

Realizing that she could get nothing here, she went on to the pastor's, to ask clarification from him.

137

He received her in his little study, which still held faint memories of a student's room in Cambridge. How much water had flowed by since their encounter beside the Koksoak! White-haired now and worn by time, the Reverend Hugh Paterson was soon to retire and doubtless that was why his eyes kept slipping away to enfold the cheerless landscape, as if it were the face of a friend who was about to leave him forever.

First of all, since he was very fond of Elsa, he took the liberty of reproaching her, in his now quavering voice, for "letting herself go."

Letting herself go or doing too much – all her life people had been accusing her of one or the other. This time she did not show too much annoyance in her eagerness to find out what this Vietnam was.

Moved by what he believed was a childish whim, the old man pulled himself to his feet and revolved the globe on his table with a touch of his hand. He indicated a spot and told her it was there.

It was a humid, very hot place, he said. Everything grew immoderately there – creepers, reeds, trees and, in the swamps, insects.

Ah, indeed! She had pictured it as a land of snow such as this because of the recollection that had come to her of blue eyes imploring her not to tell – the eyes of the young soldier in the parade or of Jimmy begging her not to betray him to the police. She was not too sure. The two pairs of eyes often blended nowadays in her memory.

For the first time in years she smiled the wide warm smile of the time when she was happy and could not conceal her happiness. Because she had sensed, as she listened to the news, that Jimmy was of the group that had just landed in Vietnam. No need to ask how but she had long been sure that he had finally joined the GI's. And now she had "seen" him arrive in Vietnam. She must have inherited this gift from Winnie who, as she grew older, had scarcely needed to disturb herself to learn of distant events that concerned her: they were simply revealed to her inwardly. And so much the better if it was warm there; Jimmy would be comfortable.

Later she had the opportunity to study some faces of Vietnam in the newspapers that reached Fort Chimo. She found them much like the faces of the people here, especially those of the women with their long dark gaze appealing from far away – they were less laughing, however, than the Eskimo faces. She began to make herself a collection of clippings showing the faces and life of Vietnam.

One day the fancy came to her that, just as his father had done on a lonely evening, Jimmy too might have drawn a shy young girl aside. The dense reeds must provide good hiding-places and the insatiable insects would swarm there also. Everything repeats itself in life. Elsa studied her collection of Vietnamese women's faces and finally chose one that especially pleased her to be the girl Jimmy had loved one evening. For all she knew, a grandson might have been born to her at the ends of the earth that she had not the slightest chance of ever seeing; all things considered, life was proving to be more preposterous and surprising than the movies had ever shown in the old days.

So she would not for anything have missed the tragic news of the world that was the source of her pleasant make-believe. She was as faithful to the news broadcasts as she was to the sunset at the edge of the immense horizon or to the river, waiting patiently for bulletins to begin, sitting at the back of the hut, her hands folded and her face open and expectant, rather as if she were at the movies or in church.

She would let it all flow over her – disasters, conflagrations, diplomatic incidents, espionage, disputes, summit meetings – without being in the least affected, waiting for some mention of Vietnam; only then did she rouse.

However, she did not know whose side she should take in this war: that of the poor GI's who were parachuted into the mysterious tropical forests – and woe betide them if they were taken alive – or that of the people of the country, so similar of feature to the people here, who were sprayed from the sky with fire.

Although she had heard talk of war all her life, she was still not quite sure what it involved. And since she had not been able to understand in the days when her mind was quick and active, how could she have done so now that it was murky from smoking and all the stories she made up for herself.

The beer she managed to buy from time to time was no help certainly. This new need, which she had acquired with her first taste, placed her, moreover, in a curious dilemma. To obtain a few cans, and in consequence a certain remoteness from life, she must first confront reality, go to the village, see people, agree to work here or there, after which it was much harder to pick up the thread of her aimless and unimpeded musings. It might be as well, then, not to disturb them in any way but it was also true that they dissipated sooner or later when they lacked for too long the kindly poison that nurtured them.

When, after drinking two or three cans of beer and smoking a whole package of cigarettes, she went out onto the beach, haggard and dull-eyed, she would feel delivered and in a sense happy. Of all the gifts of civilization none seemed to her as benificent as those that bestowed oblivion.

Always solitary, always moving along the Koksoak, she had the impression at times that she too was following the course of her life towards its ultimate goal, its end. She could even imagine that her life, born like the river far behind the old eroded mountains, had also been flowing for a sort of eternity.

She felt at times almost an impatience to "arrive" at last.

At about this time their pastor died while on a farewell visit to the most distant members of his flock and everyone agreed that no death could have suited him better than this that had sought him out at the end of the earth, in sight of the limitless sky of the tundra and committed to the memory of only three rough companions, who wept with icicles in their eyes.

His successor was quite another sort of man. He had scarcely arrived when he delivered to the handful of Eskimos assembled in the church to welcome him the most curious of sermons. They were entering upon new times, he said. The ancient barriers men had erected between themselves were crumbling. Roman Catholics, Anglicans, Jews, Methodists, and the others were all separated brothers and must strive to become one single family.

The bewildered Eskimos had great trouble grasping the difficulty of this since they had never felt separate from anyone but they prayed very willingly that the separation should come to an end if it was true that a separation existed.

However, just when the talk at church was all about uniting and praying to the same God, the Eskimos became once more the centre of the old dispute between the governments.

"These people are ours," said one government. "All the Eskimos are under our authority."

"Not at all," replied the other government. "These particular Eskimos live on our territory so they are ours."

A few unruly Eskimos then maintained that they belonged only to themselves so would the governments just leave them in peace.

This squabble was constantly under discussion in the white men's village and Elsa would return from her stints of cleaning with her head hopelessly jumbled.

One day she questioned an aged philosopher with the slightly quizzical turn of mind of the old Eskimos, whom she sometimes met on the beach, and received a most peculiar explanation.

"It's in our interest," he said, laughing briefly, "that the wrangling between our governments should continue."

"But why is that, Grandfather?"

"Because each of them will then give us more than the other so as to get us on its side."

Elsa mused over this strange situation.

"Yes, I see. But why do they want us on their side? What good will it do them?"

"Ah that!" said the old man and he raised his hands to the sky.

Having gone this far, he drifted into reflections that seemed to have no conclusion. He considered the far distance that stretched almost empty of humanity to the ice of the North Pole. There were at most two or three thousand Eskimos scattered there like a handful of seed tossed into the wind, which the wind, it went without saying, was unlikely to gather together again.

"I don't know," he said. "I've tried but I still can't see why they've become so fond of us all of a sudden."

At a moment when danger of war in the world was increasing, Elsa's little radio broke down. The silence beat upon her, making her feel forsaken, for the news of the world's woes had been a sort of company. And she much regretted not hearing about Vietnam.

But to replace the defective parts of her set, she would have had to go back to work and she was not feeling well because of a lingering attack of bronchitis, aggravated perhaps by her smoking. Since she had in any case a fair supply of tobacco, she was not pushed at least for the moment by that need and let first one week, then another, slip by in hesitation. Finally even the news of Vietnam ceased to be of much importance to her.

She began to go less and less frequently to the village, since she had obtained another big tin of tobacco in exchange for a bearskin which, now that summer had come, she imagined she would never need again. Instead, the puny silhouette was to be seen almost constantly pacing along the shore of the Koksoak. She walked with her head forward and her shoulders slumped, sometimes quite quickly, sometimes slowly and listlessly, but never stopping for very long, as if somewhere on the edge of the horizon she had a mysterious and important unknown rendezvous at which she would be more certain to arrive if she did not waste time on the way.

At forty she looked like an old woman. Grey as the earth, in one of her now colourless dresses and with unmatching shoes on her feet, considering the world with only one eye, the other closed against the smoke of her cigarette, she increasingly resembled her mother.

One day two old women who had known Winnie well, at the approach along the beach of the same silhouette, cried out with one accord, "It's not possible! But it's Winnie – Winnie come back to earth!"

As she passed Elsa heard the remark through the rhythmic sound of the waves and made an effort to straighten up so as not to resemble her mother so much, though she understood her now as never before, in her sagging flesh and in a sort of shame of the soul.

But a little later she tired and let her feet drag and her back curve again. The two old women, who had stopped to watch her and almost begun to doubt their first impression, now went off gleefully shaking their heads, "Yes indeed it was Winnie – the very image of Winnie."

Yet at just about that time, when her position in the world seemed to be the lowest, she was publicly honoured as no one among her people had ever been before.

Had he still been alive, their old pastor would have taken pleasure in recalling once again that "in love nothing is foreseeable."

18

To understand what took place, you must first know that when the people of Fort Chimo were listening to their radios they were quite often able to pick up in their cabins the voices of passers through the air. Small and at times very large aircraft flew over the region. The crew caught sight of the handful of houses below, they knew someone in the village or perhaps had a message to deliver. Or a solitary pilot was feeling bored and lonely in the clouds. For whatever reason, travellers in the sky quite often spoke words in passing to those that dwelled on earth. The event was not in itself surprising since the people were in the habit, you might say, of hearing the sky speak intimately in their ear. What shocked them this time was to hear the living and also the dead addressed by name in a voice at the outset unknown and with a pronounced American accent.

"Hello Fort Chimo," it began in general greeting.

Then, through bursts like gunfire in the microphone, came the roll of names.

"Thaddeus, dear old Thaddeus, are you still in this world and making nice little stone figures?"

The people had scarcely recovered from their surprise at hearing news asked of one of themselves, who had departed a good many years ago into that same sky, when the voice inquired of a contemporary.

"Ian," it called. "Greetings to you, Ian old fellow. And also to you the Hudson's Bay, and you the Police, and Law and Order – not to forget the schoolteacher."

Now the voice seemed to be mocking them and the people on earth felt vulnerable and insignificant. However, they thought they heard then the unmalicious laugh of someone young who was simply amusing himself.

All the while the reconnaissance plane of the US army was flying over the village, descending as low as it could as if searching for landmarks.

Among the white men in the village there were a few who possessed radio transmitters, one of them Father Eugene. The voice in the sky had scarcely launched its last volley of "greetings" when that of the Father cut in. "Who are you who seem to know everyone here?"

There was a silence followed by a blare of sound, then very far away: "Isn't that Father Eugene? How are things with you, padre?"

"Very well, thank you," replied the Father. "But surely you must be. . . ."

"An American airman come in peace," replied the voice.

"Who seems to know Fort Chimo very well."

"Fort Chimo? Could be . . . I've seen so much in my travels. And so you're still at Fort Chimo, Father Eugene?"

"And you? Where do you come from? Where are you going?"

"Hell! Where do I come from? From the war in Vietnam where I saw my share of action, believe me. Where am I going? For the moment on mission in the Arctic which gives me the occasion to fly over your interesting region."

The people listening heard what seemed to be two sighs meeting in space and then Father Eugene informed the American just back from Vietnam, "Death has had its harvest here also. Thaddeus is dead. Ian is believed to be dead. The pastor is dead. And for others things are little better. They are dying of loneliness. Have you ever thought how sad and forlorn life can be here?"

The plane did not reply for quite a long moment, having soared back high into the sky. They thought it was about to fly away, then it swooped down once more and seemed to circle over the old Quonset hut.

Suddenly it spoke again. It said with a slightly bantering sort of tenderness, "Hello, dear . . .", then two or three words were lost. Someone thought he heard, "Dear little mother. . . ." Someone else heard, "I'll see you again one of these days." Father Eugene for his part thought it was, "You'll have news from me some day."

There was no more, in any event. When the people ran outside to look at the plane, it was already out of sight.

They hurried from cabin to cabin to discuss what had happened and finally, a small excited crowd, they decided to go and congratulate Elsa.

On the way they remembered that her radio was broken and that she might well have heard nothing. What bad luck! To be greeted from high in the sky before the world and be the only one who didn't know it! Hurrying, almost running, they compared the marvellous story with one another, each adding to it according to his heart and his imagination so that it would never again be possible to recover the bare facts.

They did not find her at home, as they might have expected. With its swinging door, unmade pallet, and the old unwashed dresses hanging from a nail, the shack was so melancholy it was no wonder Elsa was almost always elsewhere. The neighbours continued their search. Just when they had such a piece of news to share with her, how like her to be wandering about in some remote spot, impossible to find.

They discovered her in a place they had already passed once without seeing her, sheltered from the wind behind a raised patch of rock, her face devoid of expression, half numbed by hours of letting her thoughts drift with the current of the river. She too had heard and seen the plane. It had come screaming over her head and had so disturbed her finally that she had turned and huddled against the rock, one arm over her head to shut out the noise.

However, from the very first words of her neighbours, it seemed to her that she had sensed a friendly presence in that plane. And she not only believed everything they told her but thought the truth must far surpass all they had remembered.

Her elation was equalled only by her keen and continuing regret that she had not been listening that day with the others.

From that moment it might be said that she lived almost entirely to have the incident described to her by those who had shared in it.

She would turn up one day in one cabin, the next day in another, hungry to hear again what had already been repeated to her many times before, hoping that some new, previously forgotten detail would be added.

So one day someone thought he recalled that the voice had made itself known with the announcement: "This is Jimmy Kumachuk speaking to Elsa Kumachuk."

At this news she fled, to enjoy it, so to speak, at her leisure, far from everyone beside the river, where she walked for hours, unable to calm an agitated excitement that kept bubbling up again.

In other cabins, however, everyone denied that the voice had identified itself and Elsa for a time kept away from these people. But a tyrannical and cruel need for truth on which to build her dreams made her return and persist.

"Are you sure he didn't give his name? Think. Try to remember."

Sometimes people who had said no the evening before, out of regard for truth, would say yes now, from a desire to give pleasure, or the other way round.

Another question she kept asking was: "From the sound of his voice, did he seem happy?"

This very simple question troubled all those who had heard the voice. Some, letting themselves be swayed perhaps by the pathetic anticipation of the mother, said yes, on the whole, the voice had seemed to them the voice of someone young and still happy and felt recompensed by seeing a return to the drawn face of some resemblance to the little Elsa of old. Others were less sure. Father Eugene shook his head. To him the boasting in the sky had suggested a youth become cynical and twisted. Elsa never went to ask for his impressions again.

On the other hand, she kept demanding particulars no one possessed: where he lived, when he would return, his address – surely he must have given his address. And why had they not paid more attention to what he said?

The marvellous event in no way astonished her. Her child, come so to speak from the sky, torn from her one day by the sky, had passed her way again in the sky; it all held together.

From her refuge beside the river she now watched with affection the flight of the rare aircraft proceeding towards the North. Some of them were only barely visible – these were loaded with bombs, said Father Eugene. She would shade her eyes from the sun and peer far into the distance after a fleeing speck of black. She imagined Jimmy up there manipulating levers to let bombs drop to their targets in a land as flat and bare perhaps as this. She could no longer believe he was untroubled by this occupation and would be crushed by the sense that she had brought him into the world to be unhappy.

She would return to the people of the village, sit down at the back of a hut, this one or that one, and resume her incessant questioning. Were they at least sure it was he? Had he said whether he would pass this way again? Whether he would some day land?

The always patient people had finally wearied of a curiosity of such persistence; they had reached the point now of answering almost anything, simply to have peace and calm her at last.

But for her it was necessary, as she said, to know what to believe, for if it was true that her child was going to return, she had no time to lose and must prepare for him, move back to the big hut, paint it and get furniture, make some curtains and a presentable dress for herself, learn how to walk on heels again, perhaps even trim up one of those old hats. At the thought of all this effort she would gaze at them in exhaustion as if asking all those assembled whether it might not be better if her child came only in dreams.

When further months and then years had passed and no one spoke of it much any more, the story acquired in people's minds the resonance of one of those evenings of old when Elsa, Mary Jane, Mildred, and Lily used to come home after the movies, all still excited, asking one another whether the images of love they had seen had been taken from the real world or simply from the imagination.

Half her teeth gone now, her back like a bent bow, her right eye screwed shut, always in a little cloud of cigarette smoke, she wandered in all sorts of weather along the shore of the wild Koksoak. Among her people, none of whom were much inclined to remain in their houses, she was considered an incorrigible nomad; almost never was she to be found at home.

Instead they would glimpse her through the fine luminous haze of the snow in the sun or struggling against gusts – a small silhouette always on the move with or against the wind.

When summer returned, there she would be again, a little more worn, a little more bowed, passing along the rim of the broad sky, parallel to that distant chain of ancient mountains that are the most abraded on earth.

At twilight it was often her way to pause in her interminable walk. She would linger and look again, deliberately, at the world in its hour of enchantment. Then she would stoop and gather up a few trifles – a pebble with a bluish sheen, a bird's egg, or some of those plant filaments, as delicate, soft, and silky as the hair of a child, that are made to carry migratory seeds far into the distance.

She would separate them strand by strand and blow upon them, her ruined face smiling to see them rise and scatter into the evening.

Afterword

BY PHYLLIS WEBB

"So what is the news of the world?" Elsa Kumachuk asks her Uncle Ian when he returns from a trip across the river to the new Fort Chimo:

> He said it was foolish beyond belief. The same little soldiers they'd seen freezing here at the time of the second world war were perhaps getting themselves soaking wet on the other side of the world, in Korea where the United States had another squabble on its hands.

By the time the novel ends, the Vietnam war has also touched this little community in the vast emptiness of northern Quebec. Gabrielle Roy's global awareness informed much of her work, but with something more than just "the news of the world." She saw, or perhaps glimpsed, like a mirage on a distant horizon, a truly human race being born, if only out of the wreckage of conflict. But what fascinated her as a writer was the flawed and varied human spectacle seen at close range.

Roy was in her fifties when she wrote *Windflower*, her experience and wisdom providing the narrator of the story with a kindly and sometimes amused omniscience. This voice, soft as windchimes, leaves us with the harmonics of sadness, our anger and outrage muted. Yet *Windflower* begins with a rape, includes incest, and probes the effects of white technology and culture on the Inuit. Who is this narrator who says, "In testimony then, here is the story, just as it is told in those parts, of Elsa, daughter of Archibald and Winnie Kumachuk"? Not an Inuit, surely – perhaps a pastor or priest, or an older white inhabitant (male? female?), for there's something condescending in that amused omniscience, guiltless, invisible.

Roy's last novel, though not her last book, *Windflower* is the second of her northern novels, the first being *The Hidden Mountain*, in which she worked out her aesthetic philosophy of "*l'artiste solitaire et solidaire.*" *Windflower* first appeared in French as *La Rivière sans repos* and included three short stories, or novellas, also dealing with technology's impact on the Inuit. Isolated, this slim volume you now hold in your hands has a poetic intensity, a formal and lyric beauty necessarily missing from a larger work such as *The Hidden Mountain*. Closer to *Where Nests the Water Hen* and *The Road Past Altamont*, yet structurally and thematically more complex, *Windflower* is unique among Roy's fiction, as distant as Ungava or a new-born star from the urban realism of her densely populated first novel *The Tin Flute*.

In this "tragic desert," this "petrified ocean" (the Inuit would see signs of life even in winter), the drama of "progress" for the Kumachuk family unfolds amid the shifting perspectives of far horizons and dingy huts, of vast sky and man-made windows, arctic sun and oil-lit lamps, the frozen sea without and "the frozen sea within," to use Kafka's phrase. And always that clear-eyed narrator controlling how events appear to us, the pace of occurrences, the modest human scale of ambitions and hopes, distancing us somewhat from the awful pain of this tragedy of acculturation, ourselves invisible, guiltless, gliding along the liquid prose, fluid even in translation. And doesn't this slim volume *feel* light? Amazing.

Elsa, Jimmy, Thaddeus, Winnie, Archibald, Ian – the names! Obviously, the English missionaries got to Fort Chimo before the French did to provide new identities, a new religion, and a new language for these ancient nomads who did not know they were so deficient. The trajectory of their story forms a sort of loop out from the nexus of the two Fort Chimos, into the drifts and blizzards of the tundra where the turning point both literally and figuratively occurs – and back along the slopes of defeat to the new. This journey from new to old and back to the future pursues the question, how to live? Given the news of the world, not to mention the news from home, this question with all its existential implications is, I think, more important than the simpler one of how to survive.

How to live? Well, we can go to the movies ("two shows a week: one for the whites, one for the Eskimos"), as Elsa and her girlfriends (Lily, Mildred, Mary Jane) have just done when the novel opens. They giggle about this horribly ugly – and funny – man, Clark Gable. And kissing! Hilarious, *disgusting*. This scene of youthful freshness and laughter (the laughter fades as the story progresses) introduces the important recurring image of the cinema and encapsulates at least two themes: the temptation and alienation of the Inuit by white culture, and the mystery and confusions of love. This scene on the fine and heavily symbolic straight road, American-built, where we've seen the girls, arms linked, pigtails flying, leads directly to the rape of Elsa by the nameless G.I. She's left puzzled and pregnant but not terribly concerned (who *is* this narrator?), the act of rape echoing the larger intensities of economic and political violations. Even southern Canadians have occasionally appeared unconcerned at uninvited attentions until the bundle of joy turns out to be a mixed blessing.

And Jimmy is mixed, and a blessing for Elsa. Arriving in mock heroic fashion like a little god, or a new star in their sky, he provides Elsa with a pretty good answer to the question how to live? Become a mother. The theatricality of his appearances in the community, the performance of the bath ritual, the costuming of this treasured blue-eyed infant, the light that surrounds his little "golden topknot" bring his mother great joy at first and a gratifying sense of purpose. Critics sometimes refer to *Windflower* as a typical Roy story of devoted motherhood, but motherhood is always problematic in her work. Despite the charming scenes of natural harmony between mother and child, especially those by the river, something is wrong, for "her soul was so preoccupied with him it had no room for anyone else." Inspired by the example of her employer Madame Beaulieu (how to live *well*), propelled by her mania for buying, buying, for washing and cleaning and doing things by the clock, disturbing the free easiness of her own family, Elsa enacts the craziness of the urban south in this desert of the north.

> Suddenly Elsa, whom no one had ever seen crying before, dissolved in tears. How odd it was to see her, once so gay, weeping, arms hanging at her sides, in the centre of the cabin.

Something is wrong – imitation, the inauthentic, seduction, loss of freedom, the cage.

The dramatic three-part structure of the novel allows for an abrupt scene shift to old Fort Chimo across the river Koksoak, site of dreams and decisions, and the emergence in Part Two of the thinking, reading, teaching Elsa. Gone the high heels, gone Madame Beaulieu's cast-off hats, the servant girl's black dress and little white crown, gone Madame Beaulieu with her incomprehensible grief. Gone the alluring plate glass window of the H.B.C. Gone Thaddeus, Winnie, and Archibald. Enter Uncle Ian to show Elsa how to live, now, by way of the past.

This scruffy idyll of the simple life places extraordinary emphasis not only on the retrieval of the past, but on intellect and spirit, on written language: the fading inscriptions in the cemetery (as in Roy's "Garden in the Wind"), Jimmy's lessons, Elsa's letter to Elizabeth Beaulieu, Ian's Bible, the reading of *Ivanhoe*, in short, on teaching, learning, and memory. Now interior and exterior spaces seem to merge; Jimmy is a calmer and happier child; something like domestic peace is achieved. As Elsa said when she found her grandmother's grave, "We came just in time." But no. Too late. "Perhaps she and her people had never become quite used to the presence among them of the police – a reminder of the endless increase of constraints."

When at the merest hint she might lose her son, Elsa fled with Jimmy to the old Fort, so now she and Ian take flight from the white policeman (nice Monsieur Beaulieu) and his law that says Jimmy must go to school. There's something almost archetypal, or perhaps just cinematic, about this escape across the tundra by dogsled in a raging blizzard, with its sexual and emotional climax. The graphically described incestuous moment in the igloo is like the last act of a dying tribe when how to survive ousts how to live.

If the reader now turned to Mordecai Richler's opus *Solomon Gursky Was Here* (1989), the change in key from Roy's gentle register to Richler's raucous croak would come as something of a shock. In Richler, nothing is sacred, not even the iconic Gabrielle Roy, for among his parade of parodies one finds the flight into the Arctic wastes replayed not just once, but twice, when Ephraim abducts his grandson Solomon and takes off with a yapping dogteam for the Polar Sea, and again when Solomon's brother and his "halfbreed" son head north in snowmobiles to administer the Jewish rites to the natives. There are nineteen years between the publication of the two books, and I think the change in sensibility is noteworthy. Richler seems immensely entertained by his garrulous characters (as we are), whereas Roy cohabits with hers in solidarity (as do we). There are no shamanic fireworks like Richler's in *Windflower*, only the steady light of Thaddeus' wisdom. I suspect this "man of conciliation and peace," this half-blind artist in stone comes close to Gabrielle Roy's own moral centre and artistic code.

In contrast to Thaddeus, Ian's chronic anger, his self-defeating isolation, his refusal to adapt to the white intruders undermine his knowledge and strength. Archibald as a character is drowned out by the sound of his machines, Winnie stalled somewhere between the old and the new, sugaring and smoking her way to extinction. All these secondary characters, with their assigned schematic functions, fill out the portrait of an indigenous community in decline. Ian disappears, the others die, even Thaddeus, as if to manifest the death of the old ways, the defeat of a people.

A return to dream time for Elsa in Part Three completes what has been called the pendulum movement of *Windflower*. Driven from one extreme to another for the sake of Jimmy, "child of mankind," she finally comes to rest in her old shack by the Koksoak, so like Winnie now, "the human being she was least anxious to resemble." Gone the years of cranking out souvenirs on her perpetual motion machine – a bitter counterpoint to Thaddeus' unhurried art – gone the spacious hut between the Anglican and Catholic missions, gone the consuming goods, bike, hockey gear, baseball bat, hamburger, gone pride, purpose, Jimmy. Even a pinball machine wouldn't have kept the morose teenager in Fort Chimo. Belonging nowhere, he takes to the air. His last words fall out of the sky like aromatic bombs.

Just as Elsa tried to turn rape into romance, so now, radio to ear, gazing into space, she transforms war into a fiction of love and regeneration, releasing the shy theme of the birth of a truly human race first uttered by old Inez in the cemetery. How to live.

We last see Elsa Kumachuk by the shores of her wild river, "a little more worn, a little more bowed," gathering a pebble here, a bird's egg there, "or some of those plant filaments, as delicate, soft and silky as the hair of a child, that are made to carry migratory seeds far into the distance." Windflower.

An Inuit telling this story would, of course, tell us another. And if some Elsa or Ian picked up this volume, would it feel so light? But I'm glad Roy risked imagining her Fort Chimoans. Mordecai Richler's parodic vision may be more in tune with his off-key times, but the expansive sympathy of Gabrielle Roy, *l'artiste solitaire et solidaire*, transmits a timeless and humane message retrieved from the news of the world.

BY GABRIELLE ROY

AUTOBIOGRAPHY
La Détresse et l'enchantement
[*Enchantment and Sorrow*] (1984)

ESSAYS AND MEMORIES
Cet été qui chantait [*Enchanted Summer*] (1972)
Fragiles Lumières de la terre
[*The Fragile Lights of Earth*] (1978)
De quoi t'ennuies-tu, Eveline?
[*What Are You Lonely For, Eveline?*] (1982)

FICTION
Bonheur d'occasion [*The Tin Flute*] (1945)
La Petite Poule d'Eau
[*Where Nests the Water Hen*] (1950)
Alexandre Chenevert [*The Cashier*] (1954)
Rue Deschambault [*Street of Riches*] (1955)
La Montagne secrète [*The Hidden Mountain*] (1961)
La Route d'Altamont [*The Road Past Altamont*] (1966)
La Rivière sans repos [*Windflower*] (1970)
Un jardin au bout du monde
[*Garden in the Wind*] (1975)
Ces enfants de ma vie [*Children of My Heart*] (1977)

FICTION FOR YOUNG ADULTS
Ma vache Bossie [*My Cow Bossie*] (1976)
Courte-Queue [*Cliptail*] (1979)
L'Espagnole et la Pékinoise
[*The Spanish and the Pekinese*] (1986)

LETTERS
Ma chère petite soeur: Lettres à Bernadette, 1943-1970
[*Letters to Bernadette*]
[ed. François Ricard] (1988)

New Canadian Library
The Best of Canadian Writing

Margaret Atwood

The Edible Woman
Afterword by Linda Hutcheon

Surfacing
Afterword by Marie-Claire Blais

Yves Beauchemin

The Alley Cat
Afterword by Kenneth Radu

Earle Birney

Turvey
Afterword by Al Purdy

Marie-Claire Blais

Mad Shadows
Afterword by Daphne Marlatt

A Season in the Life of Emmanuel
Afterword by Nicole Brossard

Fred Bodsworth

Last of the Curlews
Afterword by Graeme Gibson

Ernest Buckler

The Mountain and the Valley
Afterword by Robert Gibbs

Morley Callaghan

More Joy in Heaven
Afterword by Margaret Avison

Such Is My Beloved
Afterword by Milton Wilson

They Shall Inherit the Earth
Afterword by Ray Ellenwood

Canadian Poetry

From the Beginnings Through the First World War
Afterword by Carole Gerson and Gwendolyn Davies

Leonard Cohen

Beautiful Losers
Afterword by Stan Dragland

Ralph Connor

Glengarry School Days
Afterword by John Lennox

The Man from Glengarry
Afterword by Alison Gordon

Sara Jeannette Duncan

The Imperialist
Afterword by Janette Turner Hospital

Marian Engel

Bear
Afterword by Aritha van Herk

Sylvia Fraser

Pandora
Afterword by Lola Lemire Tostevin

NCL — A Series Worth Collecting

New Canadian Library
The Best of Canadian Writing

Mavis Gallant

The Moslem Wife and Other Stories
Afterword by Mordecai Richler

Frederick Philip Grove

Fruits of the Earth
Afterword by Rudy Wiebe

Over Prairie Trails
Afterword by Patrick Lane

A Search for America
Afterword by W.H. New

Settlers of the Marsh
Afterword by Kristjana Gunnars

T.C. Haliburton

The Clockmaker
Afterword by Robert L. McDougall

Jack Hodgins

Spit Delaney's Island
Afterword by Robert Bringhurst

Anna Brownell Jameson

Winter Studies and Summer Rambles in Canada
Afterword by Clara Thomas

Raymond Knister

White Narcissus
Afterword by Morley Callaghan

Margaret Laurence

A Bird in the House
Afterword by Isabel Huggan

The Diviners
Afterword by Timothy Findley

The Fire-Dwellers
Afterword by Sylvia Fraser

A Jest of God
Afterword by Margaret Atwood

The Prophet's Camel Bell
Afterword by Clara Thomas

The Stone Angel
Afterword by Adele Wiseman

This Side Jordan
Afterword by George Woodcock

The Tomorrow-Tamer
Afterword by Guy Vanderhaeghe

Stephen Leacock

Arcadian Adventures with the Idle Rich
Afterword by Gerald Lynch

Literary Lapses
Afterword by Robertson Davies

My Financial Career and Other Follies
Afterword by David Staines

NCL — A Series Worth Collecting

New Canadian Library
The Best of Canadian Writing

My Remarkable Uncle
Afterword by Barbara Nimmo

*Sunshine Sketches of a
Little Town*
Afterword by Jack Hodgins

Hugh MacLennan
Barometer Rising
Afterword by Alistair
MacLeod

Alistair MacLeod
*As Birds Bring Forth
the Sun and Other
Stories*
Afterword by Jane Urquhart

*The Lost Salt Gift of
Blood*
Afterword by Joyce Carol Oates

John Marlyn
Under the Ribs of Death
Afterword by Neil Bissoondath

Joyce Marshall
Any Time at All
Afterword by Timothy Findley

Rohinton Mistry
Such a Long Journey
Afterword by Alberto Manguel

L.M. Montgomery
Anne of Green Gables
Afterword by Margaret
Atwood

Emily Climbs
Afterword by Jane Urquhart

Emily of New Moon
Afterword by Alice Munro

Emily's Quest
Afterword by P.K. Page

Susanna Moodie
*Life in the Clearings
versus the Bush*
Afterword by Carol Shields

Roughing It in the Bush
Afterword by Susan Glickman

Brian Moore
*The Lonely Passion of
Judith Hearne*
Afterword by Janette Turner
Hospital

The Luck of Ginger Coffey
Afterword by Keath Fraser

Howard O'Hagan
Tay John
Afterword by Michael
Ondaatje

Michael Ondaatje
Running in the Family
Afterword by Nicole Brossard

Martha Ostenso
Wild Geese
Afterword by David Arnason

NCL — A Series Worth Collecting

New Canadian Library
The Best of Canadian Writing

David Adams Richards

Blood Ties
Afterword by Merna Summers

The Coming of Winter
Afterword by Rick Hillis

Lives of Short Duration
Afterword by Alistair
  MacLeod

John Richardson

Wacousta
Afterword by James Reaney

Mordecai Richler

*The Apprenticeship of
  Duddy Kravitz*
Afterword by David Carpenter

A Choice of Enemies
Afterword by Neil Besner

The Incomparable Atuk
Afterword by Peter Gzowski

Joshua Then and Now
Afterword by Eric Wright

St. Urbain's Horseman
Afterword by Guy
  Vanderhaeghe

Son of a Smaller Hero
Afterword by Ray Smith

Ringuet

Thirty Acres
Afterword by Antoine Sirois

Sinclair Ross

*As For Me and My
  House*
Afterword by Robert Kroetsch

*The Lamp at Noon and
  Other Stories*
Afterword by Margaret
  Laurence

Gabrielle Roy

The Cashier
Afterword by Marie-Claire
  Blais

Garden in the Wind
Afterword by Dennis Cooley

The Road Past Altamont
Afterword by Joyce Marshall

Street of Riches
Afterword by Miriam
  Waddington

The Tin Flute
Afterword by Philip Stratford

*Where Nests the Water
  Hen*
Afterword by Sandra Birdsell

Windflower
Afterword by Phyllis Webb

Ernest Thompson Seton

*Wild Animals I Have
  Known*
Afterword by David Arnason

NCL — A Series Worth Collecting

New Canadian Library
The Best of Canadian Writing

Robert Stead
  Grain
  Afterword by Laurie Ricou

Catharine Parr Traill
  *The Backwoods of
    Canada*
  Afterword by D.M.R. Bentley

Sheila Watson
  The Double Hook
  Afterword by F.T. Flahiff

Ethel Wilson
  The Equations of Love
  Afterword by Alice Munro

  Hetty Dorval
  Afterword by Northrop Frye

The Innocent Traveller
Afterword by P.K. Page

Love and Salt Water
Afterword by Anne Marriott

*Mrs. Golightly and
  Other Stories*
Afterword by David Stouck

Swamp Angel
Afterword by George
  Bowering

Adele Wiseman
  Crackpot
  Afterword by Margaret
    Laurence

NCL — A Series Worth Collecting